W9-BIQ-906

TAKE ME TO THE RIVER

TAKE ME TO THE RIVER

WILL HOBBS

SCHOLASTIC INC.
New York   Toronto   London   Auckland
Sydney   Mexico City   New Delhi   Hong Kong

No part of this publication may be reproduced, stored in a retrieval system, or transmitted in any form or by any means, electronic, mechanical, photocopying, recording, or otherwise, without written permission of the publisher. For information regarding permission, write to HarperCollins Children's Books, a division of HarperCollins Publishers, 10 East 53rd Street, New York, NY 10022.

ISBN 978-0-545-36065-4

Copyright © 2011 by Will Hobbs. All rights reserved. Published by Scholastic Inc., 557 Broadway, New York, NY 10012, by arrangement with HarperCollins Children's Books, a division of HarperCollins Publishers. SCHOLASTIC and associated logos are trademarks and/or registered trademarks of Scholastic Inc.

12 11 10 9 8 7 6 5 4 3 2 1   11 12 13 14 15 16/0

Printed in the U.S.A.   40

First Scholastic printing, April 2011

to the kids of Terlingua School

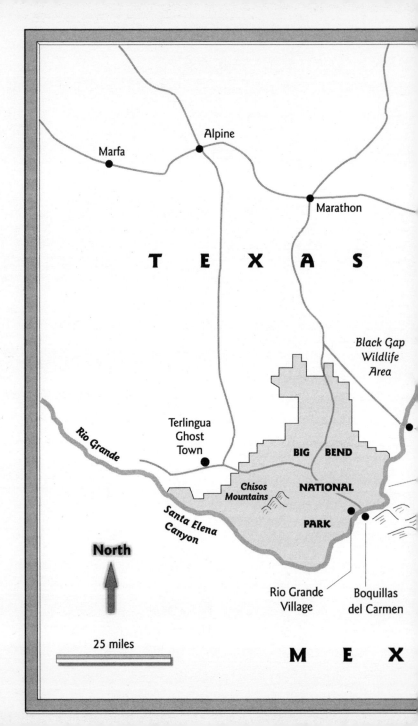

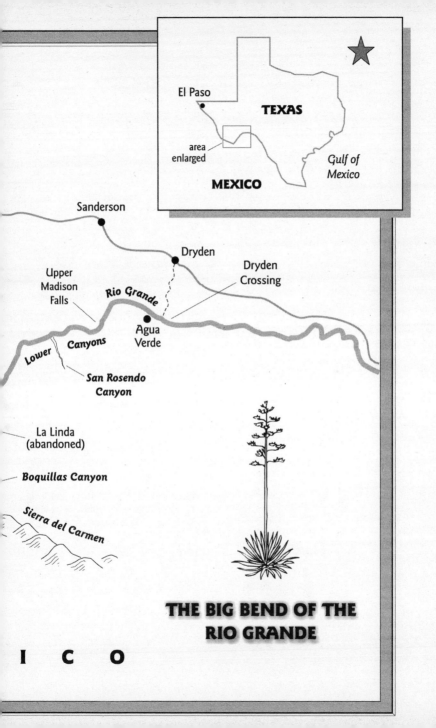

TEXAS

El Paso

area
enlarged

MEXICO

*Gulf of
Mexico*

Sanderson

Dryden

Dryden
Crossing

Upper
Madison
Falls

Rio Grande

Lower **Canyons**

Agua
Verde

**San Rosendo
Canyon**

La Linda
(abandoned)

Boquillas Canyon

Sierra del Carmen

THE BIG BEND OF THE
RIO GRANDE

I C O

Those Were His Exact Words

HOLD YOUR HORSES, I told myself. If you fly off the bus like a rabid bat, they'll turn and run.

Two plane rides and three and a half hours on a Greyhound bus, through the emptiest, most sunburned landscape I'd ever seen, and I was closing in on the town of Alpine, Texas. Alpine is where my cousin and my uncle were picking me up. There wasn't any bus service down to Terlingua, in the Big Bend, where my mother's long-lost brother made his living as a river guide.

West Texas was a thousand miles farther from home than I had ever been. I'd come all this way to paddle the fabled Rio Grande with Uncle Alan and his son, my cousin Rio. I'd never met them before, but in my imagination they had always loomed larger than life.

Strange to say, my mother hadn't seen Uncle Alan

since the year before Rio was born, and Rio was now fifteen. Her excuse? "Too many scorpions out there."

My uncle's excuse for never coming to visit us in North Carolina? Mom was sketchy on that one. I got the idea it was too expensive for him, or else he thought so little of civilization, he preferred to stay home with the scorpions.

The bus rolled on, and Alpine came into view across the high desert plain. I had pretty well guessed that the town's surroundings weren't going to look that much like the Swiss Alps. But Alpine did have mountains of a sort—scattered, scaly, and cactus clad. Pronghorn antelope were grazing below a billboard for the High Desert Hotel, which is where I would get off.

I soon had the hotel in my sights. I scanned the sidewalk and the front steps for my cousin and my uncle. I had a pretty good idea what they looked like from their annual Christmas card. "Greetings from Terlingua," it always said, over a recent picture of the two of them, canoe paddles in hand, alongside the Rio Grande. The invitation for me to come out and run the river with them came three years ago, but my parents weren't the sort to rush into things. My dad joked that if I was going to go out into the world to slay dragons, I should be of dragon-slaying age and trained in swordsmanship. Which meant that I had to wait until I was fourteen, with two years of canoe camp under my belt.

They must be waiting inside the hotel lobby, I told myself as I stepped from the air-conditioned bus into the searing heat of mid-July. Local time was six PM. I was right on the money.

Backpack and duffel bag collected, I made for the High Desert's lobby. No relatives. No big deal, I told myself, they're in a nearby grocery store. A week on the river meant twenty-one meals. Rounding up all those groceries was taking longer than they thought it would.

The lobby was deserted with the exception of a stuffed mountain lion and a rail-thin old man under a Stetson hat who rose from behind the counter to greet me. He might've been pushing ninety, with parchment skin, a nose like a hawk's beak, and piercing blue eyes. "With your permission," I said, "I just got off the bus, and I'd like to wait in your lobby. My relatives said to meet them here. They're on their way to Alpine to pick me up."

"Where from?" His voice was raspy and demanding.

"Terlingua. It's about eighty miles from here, down close to the Mexican border."

"Terlinguans are different," the old man said with attitude.

I already knew that, but given his tone, I wasn't going to admit it. To my way of thinking, that was the whole appeal. My cousin hadn't grown up like me and practically every other kid in the country. In the Age of Connectedness, my cousin and my uncle were about as unconnected as you can get. They didn't have a phone, and unbelievably, they didn't even have a computer. My mother liked to say they lived under a rock. I guess my uncle did at one time, literally. There was always a grin on Mom's face when she spoke of me going out west one day to dig them up.

What I said back to the old-timer was, "I wouldn't know if they're different, sir, I haven't met any."

"Take my word for it," he insisted.

It seemed like we had reached an impasse. I took my leave, set my duffel bag in a corner, and headed over with my backpack toward the couch and the coffee table for what I hoped would be a short wait.

The breeze stirred by the paddles of the overhead fan felt good, and the leather couch was comfortable. For a couple of impatient minutes my eyes triangulated from the front door, to my watch, to the eyes of the mountain lion lounging on a waist-high slab of burl wood across the room. From where I sat the big cat kept staring at me. Those eyes might have been made of glass, but they were making me nervous.

Maybe to avoid the mountain lion's predatory gaze, I grabbed for the newspaper on the coffee table. THREE HEADLESS BODIES FOUND IN THE RIO GRANDE, the headline read.

Well, I thought, that's not so good.

The dateline read Rio Bravo, Mexico, which reminded me that Bravo was my cousin's middle name. I didn't know much about the Rio Grande, but this much I'd picked up back home: *Rio Bravo del Norte*—Brave River of the North—is the Mexican name for the Rio Grande.

The article was only a couple of paragraphs long and added little to the splashy headline. The bodies had been discovered just the day before, and the murders were presumed to be the work of Mexico's vicious drug cartels. What I wanted to know was the location of this town of Rio Bravo. Was it in the Big Bend or anywhere close to it? I considered asking my friend behind the desk but thought better of it. Rio and his dad would know.

Sighting a computer at a table in the corner of the lobby, I checked in with my parents while the emailing was easy. I decided against mentioning the headline in the local paper. Uncle Alan had already assured them that the violence they'd been hearing about along the Rio Grande hadn't come anywhere close to the Big Bend. It was either way upstream, especially around the city of Juárez, or way downstream, closer to the Gulf of Mexico. Terlingua's river companies were running trips as usual through the canyons of the Big Bend.

What I emailed my parents was that I'd made it to Alpine and was expecting Rio and Uncle Alan any minute.

As I was finishing up with shout-outs to my younger sisters and brother, the phone was ringing behind the hotel desk. I heard the scratch of the old man's voice as he took the call. Just then some rowdy Texans emerged from the restaurant behind the lobby and drowned out all other sound. By the time they passed through onto the street, the old guy was off the phone. "Your name Dylan Sands?" he called.

"Yes, sir," I volunteered, "that would be me."

He beckoned me over. "That was your cousin calling. Left a message for you."

"They running late?"

"Not exactly. Said you should hitchhike down there."

"Hitchhike? You have to be kidding."

"Son, those were his exact words."

"What was his explanation?"

"No explanation. Oh, and one other thing. Look him up at the Starlight."

"What's that?"

"The Starlight Theatre is what he's talking about."

"Meet him at a theater?"

"It used to be one back in the mining days. That was before the market for mercury went bust and Terlingua went to ruin. The fellow who bought the ghost town put a new roof over the walls of the old theater and turned it into a restaurant."

"Did my cousin leave a callback number?"

"Nope, sure didn't."

"Did he know I was sitting right here in the lobby?"

"Sure did. I told him you was right here."

"Hmmm . . . ," I said.

The Bloody Bend

ITCHHIKE EIGHTY MILES THROUGH the desert . . . were they kidding?

I had to make a quick decision. It was nearly six thirty and I was burning daylight. Hitchhiking in the dark would be totally insane.

Better get going, I decided. My cousin and my uncle thought I could do it. Why no explanation, though?

With a quick stop at a convenience store for directions, I muttered my way five blocks east and a couple south. I planted myself beside the road sign to Big Bend National Park and Terlingua Ghost Town. Make sure to check out the driver, I reminded myself. No ax murderers. After three or four minutes a car headed my way. I stuck out my thumb, and it felt weird. This was my first time. The car passed me by.

It was seven minutes in the scorching heat before another vehicle appeared, a four-door, fire-engine-red Silverado pickup with a slide-in camper. The truck and the camper both looked new. The large man behind the wheel tilted his sunglasses and leaned forward. He studied me intently and slowed a little. He was thinking about it.

No deal—his foot was back on the gas. I gave him a forlorn smile tinged with desperation. Just then I remembered I'd forgotten to stick my thumb back out.

Thumb or no, his brake lights went on, and the truck pulled to the shoulder. I grabbed my stuff, sucking wind as I approached the back of his rig. The Texas plate—NOBEANS—wouldn't be difficult to remember. When the state trooper who found me mangled in a ditch asked if I could recall the license plate, it would be right on my lips.

"Did Dylan have any dying words?" I could hear my mother asking.

"Yes, ma'am, he did—'No beans.'"

As I came up alongside the truck, the driver lowered his window. Big guy with a round face, extra chin, and a red chili pepper on his baseball cap. His salt-and-pepper beard looked like thorny cactus needles. I didn't get a look at his eyes. His sunglasses were the mirror type favored by people with something to hide. If I lived long enough to estimate his age for the police, I would say sixty-plus. He had a belly on him, under a T-shirt that pictured a sombrero-wearing, guitar-strumming frog. Over the mariachi frog it said VIVA TERLINGUA!

With a grin, the driver said through the window, "I take it you're hitching." His accent had quite a twang to it, like he'd walked out of a cowboy movie.

"Yes, sir," I replied. He seemed friendly, but I'd had zero experience with ax murderers.

"Well, throw your stuff in the backseat and hop in before you melt!"

I did as I was told, and we headed down the road. "Nice rig," I said.

The driver groaned. "Nice rig to drive to the poorhouse. I bought it right before gas prices spiked."

"I'm glad you haven't turned the AC off for better mileage. It sure is warm out there."

"Hotter than a billy goat in a pepper patch, and hotter yet the closer we get to the Rio Grande. Between Alpine and the river, you drop three thousand foot."

My driver reached across to shake hands. "L.B. Cannon out of Killeen, Texas. Call me L.B."

I took his hand and coughed up my name. He guessed from my accent I was from eastern Tennessee, maybe Knoxville. I told him he wasn't far wrong. I was from western North Carolina, Asheville to be exact. He asked if I was headed to Terlingua and I told him I was, to look up my cousin and my uncle. Cannon gathered that this was my first time in West Texas and I told him it was. "But you've seen it in the movies," he said.

"Maybe, but not that I can think of. It looks like the far side of the moon."

"*No Country for Old Men*—did you see that one?"

"Heard of it."

"How about *There Will Be Blood*?"

"Heard of that one, too. My folks aren't too keen on violent movies."

"Violent they are, but that's true to the Big Bend, or the Bloody Bend, as it's been called."

Cannon reached for a can of chew on the console between us. "Nasty habit," he confessed as he stuck a plug between his cheek and gum. "If I'm lucky, my ticker will give out before the Big C gets me."

I asked L.B. if he was retired and he said he was. "Retired six years ago, after my better half passed away. I've been driving the blue highways ever since. Keep coming back to the Big Bend. I'm a history buff, and there's no place like it for history and scenery as far as I'm concerned. How old are you, anyway?"

"Going on fifteen."

"We used to call that fourteen," he said with amusement. "I'd be remiss if I didn't tell you that hitchhiking is a risky business at any age, but at fourteen, it's just plain stupid. Your parents in on this?"

"No way," I told him. "My mother would skin me alive." I gave him a short history of my predicament and was wrapping up as Cannon slowed to a crawl for a Border Patrol checkpoint. We weren't going to have to wait in line. We were the only vehicle on the road.

I figured they were going to stop us, but they merely eyeballed us and waved us on through.

"I guess there's no reason to check people heading

toward Mexico," I remarked.

"Oh, but there is," Cannon snorted. "For a hundred years and more, smuggling has gone *both* directions. These days, people and drugs are smuggled north, and the cash that comes from that trade is smuggled south, into the pockets of the Mexican traffickers. So are the weapons—mostly automatic weapons—that the drug cartels use to slaughter anybody that gets in their way. My camper could've been stuffed to the gills with AK-47s and millions in cash!"

"How come they didn't stop us then, and search?"

Cannon lowered his window and hawked a stream of chew, then answered my question with undisguised sarcasm. "They didn't stop us because we didn't fit the profile. The way we look. This sort of thing gravels me no end. The president of Mexico had the courage to go to war with the cartels, but he can't compete with their weaponry and the big money they use to bribe the authorities. He's begging us to stop the flow of money and weapons south, and I just got waved through? Based on what I look like and the rig I'm driving? Does that make any sense to you?"

"Not hardly."

Now was the time to bring up that headline in the local paper about the three headless guys. L.B. Cannon would know where the town of Rio Bravo was located. I asked, and he said it was "down in the valley," far downstream.

"I'm happy to hear it. I was afraid it was in the Big Bend."

"So far, so good when it comes to the Big Bend. The violence has been upriver, around Juárez, and downriver, in the Rio Grande Valley."

"Why not in the Big Bend, L.B.?"

"Ever see that NASA composite photo of the earth at night?"

"I can't say that I have."

"A dark patch indicates very little human activity. The Big Bend is part of the Chihuahuan Desert, one of the darkest areas in North America. We're talking about a vast area with very few people on either side of the river. The bad guys shy away from places that remote. Hard to do business—they would be too exposed. It's easier for them to operate in the cover of towns and cities."

"Makes sense, but I'd steer clear just based on this desert."

"People like your uncle and his boy, you gotta hand it to 'em. You really have to want to live here. The landscape might be beautiful, but it's also brutal. Look how sharp the rocks are, and near about everything that grows here is out to get you."

Cannon warmed to the subject of the bizarre-looking vegetation I was seeing out the window. In no time he had me calling out the names, like giant dagger yucca, sotol, mesquite, and creosote bush. He also pointed out landmarks as we passed them by: Double Diamond Ranch, Cathedral Mountain, Calamity Creek Wash, Butcherknife Hill, Nine Point Mesa, Fizzie Flat, Camel's Hump, the Christmas Mountains.

We were more than an hour into the drive without having passed through a town of any description. No gas stations, virtually no buildings other than a few double-wide trailers. My cousin Rio lived beyond the rim of the known world.

The sky was spectacular, with thunderheads trailing dry rain. It was so dry out here the rain actually evaporated before it hit the ground. With another bend in the road, a new mountain range soared from the desert floor. This one was so high, clouds were snagging on its tall trees and stone towers and pinnacles. This range was like one gigantic fortress, its battlements lit up by the most glorious rainbow I had seen in my life. "Unbelievable," I muttered. "What are those mountains called?"

"The Chisos. Along with the Rio Grande itself, they're the heart of the Big Bend."

At last we rolled into civilization, a town, or maybe just a haphazard collection of buildings strung along the road on the hardscrabble flats below Bee Mountain. The sign on the post office said Terlingua, but it wasn't the Terlingua I was looking for. This one had a couple of motels, the state highway department, a quilt shop, a café with gas pumps, and somewhere up ahead, the Terlingua School and a small grocery.

The cost of gas was a jaw dropper. Back home it was pushing $4.40, the worst ever. Way out here it was $5.19. At the only intersection in town, with the national park posted straight ahead, L.B. took a right. We passed between two river companies, Rio Bravo Adventures and

Blazing Paddles. It was nearly eight PM local time, and both were closed. My stomach, still on Eastern Time, was declaring mutiny. A road sign promised relief: TERLINGUA GHOST TOWN—5 MILES.

"Don't expect things to be like they are back home, like supper at suppertime," I remembered my mother telling me. What was the plan, I wondered—eat at the Starlight or at Uncle Alan's?

We were headed west, directly into the setting sun. The pavement was rough, and the road traveled the contours of the desert like a sidewinder. The sun-tortured landscape looked like it had been dumped out of a sack after the rest of the world had been made.

Burger Night at the Starlight

WE CREPT PAST THE ghost-town cemetery. The graves were mounded with bare dirt and flat stones. Rio's mother was buried here, I remembered. When Rio was only three, she died somewhere along those eighty miles I had just traveled. She was on her way back from grocery shopping in Alpine.

As we rolled past the rocky ruins of old buildings, the rounded facade of the Starlight Theatre came into view. "Where's the ghost town?" I asked.

"You're in it," Cannon replied.

"Where do people live?"

L.B. pointed at the hillside beyond. At first glance it looked more like a rock pile than anything else. On second glance, below the mine tailings that crowned the hill, small rock houses came into focus. Scattered across the slope, they were camouflaged uncannily well by giant prickly pear cactus, ocotillo, creosote bush, and half-fallen stone walls from the mining era. Vehicles were sprinkled here and there. I made out a few people moving around on foot.

Cannon hawked out the window again. "Back in the 1970s, that's when the artists and river runners and what-not started moving into the ruins. Generally people without two nickels to rub together, mostly Texans who wanted to get away from it all and didn't mind cohabitating with the snakes and scorpions. For years they had no electricity, no running water—some still live that way."

As we pulled into the Starlight's almost empty parking lot, Cannon told me that the store on the left, the Terlingua Trading Company, was the modern-day incarnation of the company store from the era when the quicksilver mines here produced nearly half the nation's mercury.

The pickup rolled to a stop. My eyes were on the Starlight in search of my cousin and my uncle. The only people in sight were two guys on the bench at the back of the long porch that connected the store and the restaurant with an art gallery in between.

L.B. wished me luck as he drove out. The two men at the back of the porch came to the rail, not to greet me, but to gaze into the distance.

I turned around to see what they were looking at, and there were the Chisos Mountains, bigger than life and all lit up by the setting sun, their battlements aglow with brilliant reds and golds.

I climbed the steps to the porch, dropped my stuff on the bench, and went into the restaurant. This time I was keeping my expectations in check. Something told me this wasn't going to work out, either. Maybe there would be another message.

Folding metal chairs, concrete floor . . . there was nothing fancy about the Starlight, but it was loaded with atmosphere. I felt like I was five hundred miles deep into Mexico, in the time of Pancho Villa. The plastered walls were watermelon red giving way to mango gold. If I wasn't mistaken, some of the plaster was pocked with bullet holes. Up toward the ceiling, the plaster had fallen away, revealing the bare stones. The walls had to be massively thick to be able to soar that high and support the rafters running clear across. "On the Road Again" was playing on the PA to a nearly empty house. Only three tables had customers, and the bar stools were empty.

I stayed planted for a minute just inside the front door. I was thinking of what to do when a lanky kid with shaggy brown hair appeared at the kitchen doorway. He was wearing an apron. At first I wasn't positive it was him. This kid looked like he might be older than Rio's fifteen, and was taller and more muscled than I was expecting.

Yep, it was Rio. Soon as he had me spotted, my cousin broke into a big smile and gave a couple of fist pumps. He called my name as he was closing in, and I called his. He grabbed me with a bear hug. I was pretty well shell-shocked.

"I can't believe it!" Rio exclaimed. "I can't believe you're actually here!"

"Me neither. You've shot up since your last Christmas card."

I looked around for my uncle, but I didn't spy any candidates. "It's been a long day," I said.

"I'm so glad that you came, Dylan."

What came out of my mouth in return was, "Can I still get something to eat?"

"Not a problem. I was hoping you'd get here before closing. It's two-for-one burger night."

"But you're working, right?"

"My boss said he would finish the dishwashing when you got here." Rio took off the apron, folded it, and placed it on the side of the bar. "No more pearl diving until August."

Rio led the way to a table. I asked if my backpack and duffel were okay where they were, outside on the bench.

"Sure thing—this is Terlingua."

Just then a very attractive waitress came around from behind the bar and headed our way. She was my mother's age, but she didn't dress anything like my mother. She wore black, with lots of silver and lots of style. "Howdy, boys," she said. "Who's your friend, Rio?"

"This is Dylan, my river-crazy cousin from North Carolina."

The lady gave me a big smile. "Lot of rivers back in North Carolina, Dylan?"

"Yes, ma'am, and lots of trees."

"Been out here before?"

"No, ma'am, I haven't."

"What does it look like to you?"

"Huge. Empty. Dry. Snakebit, I guess."

"Never heard it put better."

By this time I could have eaten the menus for an appetizer, except the waitress had them tucked under her elbow. Rio looked at me strangely, like I was staring at the lady's elbow, then introduced her. Ariel was her name. She was his neighbor in the ghost town, and she was also an artist.

Ariel asked if we were up for the two-for-one burgers with fries. Rio recommended the guacamole topping. "Perfect," I said. We both ordered large Cokes.

"Back to our trip," I said. "I Googled four different canyons in Big Bend. What stretch of the river are you and your dad talking about?"

"We were going to do the Lower Canyons."

"Now we're going to paddle somewhere else?"

All of a sudden, Rio looked real uncomfortable. "Guess I might as well spit it out. My dad isn't around."

"Where is he?"

"He took off a few days ago for Alaska."

Underwhelmed

"ALASKA?" I SAID. "YOU'RE putting me on."

"I wish I was. It came up really fast, Dylan. My dad said to tell you how disappointed he was, after expecting to finally meet you and run the river with you. He didn't really have a choice."

I was awfully slow to process what I'd just heard. It was like I'd suffered a concussion.

"He asked me to explain, Dylan. Dad thought he was going to be able to work here this summer, guiding on the Rio Grande. Even though the river runs highest in the summer—when the rains come—summer is the low season for the river companies. The tourists aren't too keen on the heat. Most of the guides leave to work on rivers in Colorado, where it's nice and cool. As of last week Dad was the only guide left in town, but he thought he had work. He had three bookings in August lined up for after our trip."

Rio's eyes were flitting this way and that with barely a bounce off mine. He took a quick breath and kept talking. "The economy is killing us, Dylan, especially the cost of gas, and the fear factor about Mexico isn't helping. Tourist visits to Big Bend National Park are way down, and business for the river companies has cratered. Those three bookings for August I just told you about, they all canceled. My dad found out only four days ago. Well, he had to get work, and fast. It's always hand-to-mouth around here. An old friend who owns a river company out of Haines, Alaska, offered three trips on the Alsek River—each one eleven days long—if he could get there in twenty-four hours. Dad threw some stuff in a bag, drove to El Paso, and jumped on a plane. He's going to make some good money up there."

Rio leaned back, waiting for me to say something. I was still too dumbfounded, just trying to stay calm and not say anything I would regret.

"I know, Dylan. This sucks."

Ariel brought our burgers, two apiece. They were huge and looked delicious, but as I started in on the first one, I was so distracted by the grinding of my mental gears I couldn't even taste it.

I was hungry, though. I kept chewing and swallowing. Between burgers I said, "How come you didn't let me know before I left home?"

"My dad was on the fly. He asked me to take care of it

and I told him I would . . . I came down here to the Starlight and started to punch up your number. I just couldn't do it."

"Uh, why not?"

"Well, I knew your bag was probably already packed."

"It was, but still—"

"What I mean is, I knew how much you were counting on it. I was counting on it myself, like you wouldn't believe. Summer around here is deadly dull. The kids from school are scattered all over the desert. There aren't any even close to my age who live in the ghost town. I figured we could go ahead and have a great time doing whatever."

"You could've told me when you called the hotel in Alpine. I mean, I was right there."

"I know. I'm really sorry about that. I figured that if I filled you in, you would've phoned home and that would've been the end of it. Don't you think?"

"Probably so."

"Look, I'm really sorry. I'll understand if you scratch and do a U-turn. I can see how annoyed you are."

"More like disappointed."

"I thought the chance might never come again. You know how long we've been talking about it. Well, not literally. You know what I mean."

"Your dad actually left you here for more than a month, alone?"

"He was away for a month last summer, working in Colorado. It's not as bad as it sounds."

"It's not?"

"It's not easy, but I can handle it. And people in the ghost town look out for each other. Really, I'm sorry. I had this whole image of how it was going to be. I realize how weird this must seem."

I was at a loss as I tried to sort out my feelings about his deception. Here's what made it so difficult: My cousin seemed so sincere and so *honest*, if that's the right word.

One thing Rio was right about—how long we'd been looking forward to this. He might be correct, too, that it was now or never. My mother thought of her brother as flaky enough as it was. Would she be willing to make like this snafu didn't happen and try again the following summer? Send me all the way back to run the river?

Maybe not. Well, probably not.

"Don't beat yourself up," I told my cousin. "I understand, sort of. What will we do if I stay, besides hang out?"

"We can paddle Santa Elena Canyon for sure. It's the closest and shortest of the four canyons. The put-in is only ten miles away. Ariel can drop us off and pick us up. The canyon is real narrow, real deep—an incredible place."

"Lots of rapids?"

"Only one, called Rock Slide, but it's a big deal."

"How long of a trip is it?"

"Just one day . . . you look disappointed."

"I guess I am. I mean, we were going to have a week on the river, and that sounded awesome. But, okay, we could paddle Santa Elena Canyon for a day—then what?"

"We could do a lot of mountain biking . . ."

"I'll have to sleep on it," I said. "Sleep on the whole deal."

"Fair enough."

On our way out of the Starlight, we collected my stuff off the porch. Rio asked if I wanted to climb to the top of the hill by the water tower and throw fireworks into an eight-hundred-foot-deep mineshaft. The fireworks bouncing off the walls all the way down made for "an insanely spectacular show."

I was dead tired and asked for a rain check. I followed Rio across the hillside into the residential part of the ghost town. There weren't any streetlights but the moon was up. My cousin told me to watch where I stepped; the rattlesnakes were active at night. Lights twinkled here and there from dwellings scattered amid the ruins. I felt like I was sleepwalking in a postapocalyptic world.

We came to an iron gate in a stone wall. The gate squeaked open to a patio and Rio's front door. I took note that my mother's brother and his son didn't live under a rock after all, though their house was made out of rocks. "Welcome," Rio said. *"Mi casa es su casa."*

5

Kissed by an Assassin

THE HOUSE WAS SMALL, with only two bedrooms, a small living room, and a small kitchen/dining room. Rio showed me to my crash-landing site, his father's bedroom. I made a thorough search for scorpions, even pulling back the sheet. Just in case, I got my camping flashlight out of my stuff and placed it on the nightstand before I turned out the light and got into bed.

I slept like the dead until I was awakened by the rapid beating of my heart. The room was pitch-dark. It was the middle of the night.

I flicked the flashlight on, pointed it all around. Not a scorpion in sight. My heart was still racing. Bad dream? Suddenly I remembered: bad dream, indeed, and it came rushing back. I was perched at the edge of a vertical mine-shaft while Rio was lighting Roman candles and tossing them in. Suddenly I had lost my grip, and was falling, falling, falling.

Now that I was awake, my lower lip was itching something awful. I kept touching the spot to try to figure out what that was about. It was all I could do not to scratch it. At last my weariness won out and I was able to fall back asleep.

I slept well enough until the stillness of the night was shattered with what sounded like the wails of a lunatic. I bolted upright like a caveman with a lion at his throat. What was it, and where was I?

As the wails were followed by yips and barks, I came up with the answers, which were (A) coyote, and (B) my flaky uncle's place in Terlingua, Texas.

It was a quarter after five. Dawn was beginning to filter through the screen window along with the bedlam. My lip still itched, and it felt swollen. I tried to get back to sleep but no such luck. Half an hour later the lunatic coyote was still carrying on.

Rio had left the door to the bedroom open so the cool air entering through the screens could circulate through the house. A coffeepot began to burble.

The bathroom was attached to the house, but you had to go out the front door to get there. "There'll probably be a scorpion in the sink," Rio called as I stumbled out the open front door. "Go ahead and annihilate it."

His prediction proved correct. I looked for a weapon and found a book on the back of the composting toilet. It was entitled *The World Without Us*. No doubt it said that scorpions would do nicely in a world without people. "This one won't get the chance," I muttered as I mashed it with the spine of the book.

The scorpion dispatched, I checked myself out in the mirror. My lip was swollen something awful. I washed my face and hands with less water than my mother uses on one of her African violets. A gallon or two was all you really needed for a shower, Rio had told me the night before. The ghost town had finally gotten a water supply, but his house wasn't hooked up to it. Too expensive, Rio said. They collected rainwater from the roof and hauled water when their cisterns ran dry.

Rio and his dad had enough electricity to power the lights, the stereo, a TV, and a DVD player. They didn't actually get TV; the TV was for watching DVDs. The electricity came from solar panels on the hillside behind the house. They cooked on propane; their fridge and their hot water heater also ran on propane.

As I returned from the bathroom along the edge of the flagstone patio, I was keeping my eyes down on account of my bare feet and the scorpions. I didn't see any, but I did notice a huge, hairy tarantula climbing onto the threshold of the open door.

"Annihilate it?" I asked. Rio was sipping coffee from a Mexican mug and watching the arachnid come in.

"No way," he said. "That's Roxanne."

I soon learned that tarantulas make excellent house-guests, are virtually harmless, and pay for their lodging by eating insects, flies, conenose bugs, and sometimes scorpions. "I'll show you what happens if I put her out," Rio said. He carried Roxanne outside on the palm of his hand and gently set her down on the far side of the patio. "You drink coffee?" Rio asked as he returned.

"Not really. Gimme some."

We sat at the kitchen table, drank Zapatista Blend, and watched the huge black spider turn herself around. She began to march back to the front door. Rio said that a tarantula moving indoors was a sign that the thunderstorms would come soon.

This was going to take a while. Roxanne lifted only one foot at a time. I gained an insight into how Rio entertained himself.

You wouldn't have known this house had been resurrected from a ruin. The thick stone walls were plastered smooth and painted white as cream. The window frames were turquoise blue. The floors were smooth concrete with a light blue tint.

We took our coffee mugs and a couple of bagels outdoors to a patio table under a "ramada," as Rio called it, a shade break of thatch supported by four poles. This early, we weren't in dire need of shade. The morning air was almost too cool for T-shirts and shorts. I let out a massive yawn and said, "I could've slept another six hours."

Rio shrugged. "If you don't have AC, you have to take advantage of the cool part of the day or you'll go mental."

My finger went to my swollen lip. "Conenose bug got you," Rio said. "It's also known as Mexican bedbug, or assassin bug. Nasty sucker."

"I didn't see any. Are they tiny?"

"Not at all. They're half an inch long, sometimes longer. Mostly they prey on insects. Their long beak injects saliva with a toxin that dissolves tissue, then sucks the insides out of the insect."

"Your assassin bug mistook my lip for an insect?"

"Unfortunately, they also snack on mammals. With humans, they usually go for the lips, which is why they're also known as kissing bugs. They're a royal pain. You never know when it's happening because the first thing they do is inject an anesthetic. Something else they inject makes your heart start racing, but only when they're done and gone. That's when you wake up."

Just then, the sun began to rise over the Chisos Mountains. The first rays fell on a covey of quail darting across the flagstones behind Roxanne, who was climbing over the doorsill again. A roadrunner with a lizard in its mouth ran the length of the low wall that ringed the patio. It was the first I'd seen outside of a cartoon.

We headed back to the house for more coffee, not that I needed any. Stepping over Roxanne, who was headed for the bookcases, I checked out the art and photos on the walls while Rio was pouring. What caught my eye first was a piece of art the likes of which I'd never seen—a large hubcap painted in bright acrylics with a geometric design around the outside and a river scene at the center. A Mexican boy was sitting on a ledge and watching the Rio Grande as it wound through a canyon.

My eye caught the signature at the bottom of the

hubcap. "Ariel painted this!"

"I told you she was an artist. Her hubcaps are all over West Texas."

We started in on some cold cereal. A spiral-bound guidebook on the bookcase caught my eye, the mile-by-mile guide to the Lower Canyons of the Rio Grande. This was the section of the river I'd come out to paddle. I jumped up and brought it back to the table.

The guidebook contained photographs of canoes running the biggest rapids. I was riveted, but it was a tantalizing what might have been.

Rio wasn't saying a thing, which was understandable under the circumstances. As I set it aside I said, "Those Lower Canyons look plenty challenging. It would've been a blast. Sorry if I drooled all over your book."

Rio had a look in his eye. "Maybe we can still go for it."

"Really? How's that? You got my attention."

"It's a week-long trip . . . wouldn't that be awesome, just the two of us?"

"No question," I said, putting aside for the time being my first thought, which had to do with my parents. "You really think we could?"

"I don't see why not. The only problem is, I don't have enough money saved up. I could swing the groceries, but there's a lot of driving involved. Another one of Ariel's gigs is driving shuttles . . . I'm thinking she might help us out if we could pay her gas."

"I brought some spending money. How much gas money are we talking about?"

Rio grabbed a map and put pencil to paper. Around two hundred dollars was the answer. Ariel's round-trip driving on the front end would be 120 miles. The round-trip at the back end would add another 300 miles. I told my cousin I was good for the gas money.

"Is your bus ticket already paid for?"

"Same as the airline ticket. Both were round-trips."

"Grab your flip-flops. I'll show you our stuff."

Rio led me out to the shed behind the house where they kept their river gear: a raft with frame and oars, coolers and propane bottles, life jackets, watertight food boxes, "dry bags" for storing personal gear, and on and on. The canoes were real beauties, sixteen-foot expedition-type Mad Rivers that flared widely through the middle for high-volume loads. Both bow and stern had a curving lift built into them, like the ends of a rocking chair leg, to deflect incoming whitewater. "You think your dad would be cool with it?" I asked. "Us going by ourselves?"

"I've been thinking about that. Yeah, I do. What about your folks?"

"I'd have some explaining to do. . . . They've been talking about me making independent decisions and suchlike. They know how hard I've worked for it. They knew it would be an adventure."

"It would be an adventure, that's for sure. Your call, Dylan."

I told him I was leaning strongly in favor.

It was a three-minute walk to Ariel's place, a school bus. Painted with colorful desert scenes, it was a real eye-catcher. Ariel was outside, painting a hubcap under a ramada like the one shading Rio's patio table. She said she'd be happy to help us out with the driving.

The hubcap artist asked if we wanted to use her email. I took it she was talking about me running everything by my parents. Asking their permission, that is.

Inside Ariel's bus, which was beautifully tricked out, my head was spinning. I wasn't in any hurry to jump on the computer.

Rio could see I had a whole lot on my mind. He sat down to check the weather forecast and email some friends. I figured this was how he'd been emailing me. I went outside to sound out Ariel about my cousin. I asked how come she was confident about Rio and me heading off on our own.

"Rio is in his element when he's on the river," she told me. "I know. I'm an old river guide myself. If you two hang around the ghost town instead and bicycle up and down the highway and mess around near the mineshafts like kids do, that would be more dicey, in my opinion."

Not to mention, I thought, that on the river I would be sleeping inside a zippered tent and not in my uncle's bed with assassin bugs. "Thanks," I said. "That's what I wanted to hear."

Rio came out of the bus. "Your turn," he said. I went inside and emailed a message home. I told them that everything was great. I left out certain details like any mention of Rio's father or his whereabouts. I said we'd be going on the river soon.

6

Take Me to the River

BEFORE NOON THE NEXT day, Rio and I were on the road to adventure with Ariel at the wheel of her relic of a pickup. We were going to bite off even more of the river than we talked about at first. Not only were we going to run the Lower Canyons, we had tacked on three days upstream for a total of ten days.

Why three more days? That was Ariel's idea, and we were happy to oblige. On our first day we were going to drop some donated supplies at a Mexican village called Boquillas del Carmen. It was all good, according to Rio. After dropping the donations, we would run Boquillas Canyon, a spectacular section of the river I would have missed had we started our trip downriver, at the put-in for the Lower Canyons.

Our sixty-mile drive to the river skirted the Chisos

Mountains on their north side, then dropped into a starker and starker landscape dominated by creosote bush and by ocotillo, which resembled buggy whips. We were going to intercept the Rio Grande at a place called Rio Grande Village, in a far corner of Big Bend National Park.

Ariel's old pickup didn't have AC. The heat was so intense, we had to keep the windows down and blast air through the cab by opening the fins on both sides. Conversation was impossible. As the miles rolled by I was left alone with my thoughts, which were up and down and all over the place.

I had a queasy feeling in the pit of my stomach, and it wasn't from something I ate. This wasn't anything like I'd been picturing this trip since forever, like my parents were picturing it right now, with my uncle along. I was in uncharted territory in more ways than one. I hadn't told my parents any lies, but I hadn't told them the truth, which pretty much amounted to the same thing. Would they have given me the green light, knowing it was going to be just me and Rio?

The chances of that were slim to none.

I hated the way this felt. It felt like I was starting down a slippery slope. To have come this far, though, only to turn back and go home—that would be totally unacceptable.

Before any river trip, you get the jitters. Man, did I have them now. I felt like asking Ariel to stop the truck so I could throw up on the side of the road.

Ariel picked up on my state of mind. "Nervous?" she

asked me, almost shouting. I was right at her side, sand-wiched between her and Rio.

"I always get some butterflies," I admitted.

"That's good, that's normal. These canyons are something special. You guys are going to have an awesome trip."

"Hope so," I said.

A few miles on, and something new came into view. Between us and a soaring mountain range, a winding strip of bright green vegetation marked the course of a river. I let out a whoop when Rio confirmed it was the Rio Grande. I could feel my adrenaline jets beginning to fire. There is nothing, absolutely nothing, that beats moving water.

As Ariel drove into Rio Grande Village, Rio explained that it wasn't much of a village. For the sake of the tourists, Big Bend National Park had a campground here, a visitors' center, and a general store that sold gas and groceries. At midsummer, with the temperature around a hundred every day and the price of gas having soared out of sight, we found it virtually deserted. There were only two RVs parked in the cottonwood-shaded campground.

I ran up a trail to a hilltop for my first look at the river. Rio was on my heels, and Ariel was following at a walk. Once I got to the overlook, I didn't know what to make of what I was seeing. This couldn't be the Rio Grande. It looked more like a drainage ditch. "Uh, where's the river?" I asked my cousin.

"You're looking at it," he replied.

The riverbed was fifty yards wide, but mostly dry. The river itself was less than fifty feet wide and mostly ankle deep. At its deepest it might have come up to your knees. The water was pea green, not my favorite color, with no discernible current. "C'mon, you're kidding," I said. "This is a side channel, right?"

"Afraid not. That's the Rio Grande."

"I thought you said that the river runs highest in the summer."

"When it rains. July and August are our rainy season, but the rains haven't started yet."

By now Ariel had joined us on the hilltop. I wasn't going to say a thing more about the river. I could pretty well guess I'd already ruffled my cousin's pride. I knew the Rio Grande wasn't going to look like the rivers back home, but this was pathetic. How we were going to go a hundred and sixteen miles in ten days, I had no idea.

The low flow must have looked so normal to Ariel, she didn't even mention it. What she was keen to point out to me was the Mexican village where Rio and I were going to drop the donations. Even with my dark sunglasses cutting the glare, it was hard to spot. Finally I made it out, shimmering in the heat, a couple miles downriver. "Bo-KEY-us" was how she pronounced it. Boquillas sat at the foot of the soaring mountains called the Sierra del Carmen.

The stuff we were going to drop off included used laptops for the village school, some empty propane bottles that couldn't be filled on this side of the river for some reason, half a dozen small motors reclaimed from exercise treadmills, a secondhand solar cell, an old sewing machine, and half a dozen trash bags full of fabric scraps that the women of the village would turn into quilts. It was okay to take donations across the border without going through a customs station as long as they had hardly any resale value.

We had some work to do if we were going to reach the village before dark. We were about to start down the path to Ariel's truck when we heard the distant *chop-chop-chop* of helicopters.

"Border Patrol?" I wondered aloud.

The helicopters were getting ever louder. Rio had them spotted, but I hadn't yet. "Unreal!" he shouted. "Those are U.S. Army!"

Rio was pointing north of the Chisos Mountains. Now I saw them. The helicopters, half a dozen of them, were flying low, along the route of the road we had just traveled. They were coming fast, with a whirring thunder like a breaking storm. These were serious war machines— attack helicopters. "Black Hawks!" I shouted over the din. "I've seen them back home at Camp Lejeune!"

"They're heading for Rio Grande Village!" Rio shouted back.

They sure enough were. The Black Hawks circled the campground a couple of times. Twice, they passed within a hundred yards of our hilltop. The side doors of the choppers were open, with soldiers at their battle stations manning machine guns. We caught some heavy downdraft; the roar was deafening.

The gunships pulled back to allow even more helicopters to approach the river—three giant Chinooks, made for hauling troops and fuel and supplies.

The Chinooks hovered just short of the river as the Black Hawks circled them protectively. We watched the three Chinooks put down in the Park Service campground, in a clearing only a stone's throw from those two RVs.

The Black Hawks didn't follow them in. To our amazement, the gunships raced across the river and into Mexico.

"Mercy!" Ariel cried.

At first I wondered if they were heading for the village across the river, but within minutes, they were far beyond Boquillas and miles into Mexico.

The Black Hawks were gaining altitude rapidly, flying up and up, in the direction of the Sierra del Carmen. It looked for all the world like they were going to smack into the cliffs. It wasn't long before they crested the forest atop the range and blinked out of view.

It crossed my mind that maybe this wasn't such a good time to be spending ten days on the Mexican border.

Good-bye, Good Luck!

ARIEL DROVE TOWARD THE visitors' center to find out what in the world was going on. We didn't get that far. The park ranger had jumped in his truck and raced to the campground where the big Chinooks had landed. He was already engaged in what looked like dead-serious conversation with an army officer. Behind them, three dozen soldiers were already at work unloading the helicopters.

We waited fifteen minutes before Ariel got her chance to speak with the park ranger. They knew each other by name; they were old friends. The ranger hadn't known the helicopters were coming. The army had chosen Rio Grande Village as a forward base for some kind of operation in Mexico that they weren't authorized to discuss, except to say it was in cooperation with the Mexican government and military. The ranger had been told to close the entrance and notify campers to leave ASAP.

"Can we still launch a river trip?" Ariel asked the ranger.

The answer was yes, as long as we did it "expeditiously."

"What about the store?" was Ariel's next question. "Is the store still open?"

"You might run over there real quick. My guess is, it won't be for long."

We piled back in the truck like our hair was on fire and raced for the store. What with a number of far-flung stops we'd made that morning to pick up the donations for Boquillas, the one-man grocery in Terlingua had closed for lunch hour before we got there. "No problem," Rio had said. "We'll shop in Rio Grande Village. They can use the business."

Those fifteen minutes we had just lost waiting to talk to the park ranger turned around and bit us. The parking lot in front of the store was plumb empty as we drove in. A sign on the door, hastily scrawled with a black marker, read, CLOSED INDEFINITELY.

Hmmm . . . , I thought.

We looked down the road that led out of Rio Grande Village. Dust was still hanging in the air from a vehicle leaving in a hurry.

"Just missed him," Ariel said. "This summer has been a disaster for the concessionaires in the park. I guess he was thrilled to have an excuse to shut down. We could head home, boys, and try again tomorrow."

"We could," Rio allowed, "but the army wouldn't let us back in. Our only shot at dropping your donations and floating Boquillas Canyon is if we launch this afternoon. We've got enough groceries in the truck. It's not like we're going to starve."

The groceries Rio was alluding to were the sum total of the canned goods and boxed food, spices, cooking oil, and so on that he had at home. To keep the grocery bill down, he brought it all along. "What do you think, Dylan? Think we can get by?"

I allowed that I figured we could. I felt a lot better when Ariel said we could have the emergency food stowed behind the front seat of her truck, which turned out to be three cans of Spam, three cans of tuna, and a twelve-pack of energy bars. A lot of the locals carried emergency rations, I learned, not so much for themselves as for the illegal crossers they sometimes encountered on the back roads.

"I brought some fishing gear along," Rio added. "I'd say we're good to go."

Ariel put her truck in gear and we headed for the put-in. There's nothing like nearly having something snatched away to make you want it all the more.

On our left, soldiers were unloading fuel drums out of the big Chinooks. Other soldiers were erecting sleeping tents. A much bigger tent was also going up—a mess hall, maybe? Ariel backed her truck close to the river at the launch site, a bulldozed cut in the riverbank.

Ariel retreated to the shade of a cottonwood as Rio and I fell to unloading the truck. We began by undoing the canoe's tie-downs and sliding it down from the carry racks. We tumbled the raft out of the back of the bed and rolled it aside. I couldn't help eyeing the raft like it was a rogue elephant. Since forever I had pictured Rio and me in canoes, paddling the Rio Grande side by side. I said as much that morning, back at the ghost town, when we were loading up.

"If we were only out for a few days, that would be the way to go," my cousin agreed. "But for ten days, that's different. If it really gets to raining, the river could get too big for a canoe to handle."

"How likely is that?" I insisted.

"You never know," he answered with a shrug. "Safety first. It's what my dad would do. He's seen it happen."

"If it did happen, we would both continue on in the raft?"

"Yep. Stash the canoe and come back for it later."

Eyeballing the so-called river as we pumped up the raft, I had my doubts as to how far we would get before Rio had to jump out and drag it.

Once everything was off the truck, Ariel drove back to the visitors' center to get us a river permit to fill out.

Rio and I were putting the rowing frame together when a couple of soldiers headed our way. They were dressed in desert camo and were carrying automatic weapons. I was afraid they were going to put the kibosh on our trip.

The one with four stripes did the talking. The other,

with two stripes, was along for the ride like me. The sergeant's mission was to find out how soon we could vacate the premises. Rio assured him we would be on the river shortly. "Good," the sergeant said. "How long will you boys be out?"

"Ten days—how come?"

"There's a possibility that the Big Bend is in for a major weather event within that time frame."

Rio's eyebrows knitted doubtfully. "Are you positive, sir? I checked the ten-day forecast yesterday, and it wasn't calling for a major weather event."

"That forecast might be subject to change. There's a hurricane by the name of Dolly entering the Gulf of Mexico later today. This morning it was brushing the tip of the Yucatán. The computer models show landfall three days from now, most likely on the East Texas coast or western Louisiana. Here's a heads-up for you: There's a one in ten chance of Dolly coming ashore in the Brownsville area, at the mouth of the Rio Grande."

"One in ten, that's not very likely."

"If she does, and she happens to follow the river upstream, we might see some heavy precipitation."

"Thanks for the heads-up. One more thing . . . Can you tell us anything about your mission, Sergeant? Why your unit's Black Hawks flew into Mexico?"

"Sorry, I'm not authorized."

"Mexico is having a big battle with the drug cartels, and they needed our help?"

The faint suggestion of a smile crossed the sergeant's

lips. "Have a good trip," he said in parting.

"Think we might make the acquaintance of Dolly?" I asked Rio as we watched them go.

"We're in the eleventh year of a drought. I'd almost like to see a tropical storm come our way."

We went back to rigging the raft. By the time Ariel returned with the permit we had it fully rigged, with our trip gear stowed either in the rowing compartment or in the back. The stuff for Boquillas we piled haphazardly in the front. Across the river, the forested crest of the Sierra del Carmen was turning dark. Rio said there was a good chance we were in for a thunderstorm this very day.

Rio sat down and filled out the permit with our names and addresses, description of boats, and itinerary. The Park Service managed the use of the river in the park and the "wild and scenic" corridor below. I was relieved that someone besides Ariel was going to know what we were up to in case we went missing.

It was time to say good-bye. We made sure we were in sync with Ariel about our rendezvous. We were going to spend nine nights on the river. At noon on the tenth day she would meet us at a place called Dryden Crossing at the end of a remote ranch road.

"You guys sure enough look like desert river rats," Ariel said. And we did, with our sunglasses and wide-brimmed straw hats, our river knives deployed heart-high on our life jackets, our arms and legs protected with super-light long sleeves and trousers. Our feet were clad with sneakers rather than river flops on account of the hostile terrain.

We thanked Ariel for everything she had done for us. "Take care of each other, you guys," she said, all misty-eyed, and gave us big hugs. We promised we would.

Rio waded into the river, hopped aboard the raft, and took the oars. I waded out with the canoe and stepped inside. I reached for the paddle and took my first stroke. "Good-bye, good luck!" Ariel called as we headed around the bend.

Uh, I Don't Think So

BEFORE WE'D EVEN FLOATED the length of the cotton-wood trees in front of the helicopters, Rio had to get out and pull his raft over a sandbar. The canoe had a much shallower draft. For the time being, I was able to stay in my seat.

Pretty quick Rio found a little more water to work with and was rowing downstream. I followed, trying to wrap my mind around the fact that the midpoint of this creeklike river was an international boundary. At the moment, both shores were covered with cane grass that soared up to fifteen feet. Mexico didn't look a lick different from the United States.

The wind picked up. The cane was dry, and the wind made it chatter. A stiff gust blew the raft onto another sandbar. Rio put on a pair of gloves like he meant business. He jumped out with a splash and horsed the blue raft, a fourteen-footer, down the river. It would've been even harder to drag the raft if he hadn't put some of the heaviest stuff in the canoe, including all three five-gallon jugs of drinking water and a small cooler full of our canned goods.

After fifty yards, Rio was drenched in sweat. I thought for sure he'd have to give up. He put his head down and pulled harder. When he stopped to catch his breath again he told me we were lucky to have this much water—Colorado and New Mexico take the lion's share. We would be walking on a dry riverbed if not for a Mexican river called the Rio Conchos, which flowed into the Rio Grande not very far upstream of the Big Bend.

At last Rio found water deep enough to float the raft and was back in the rowing seat, gulping water from one of our one-gallon bottles. I took a slug, too. In the heat, it was nearly hot as tea. With his back against the wind and pulling downstream, Rio made some extremely hard-won progress. At the rate we were going, though, even covering the two miles down to the village before dark seemed unlikely.

Next time Rio got stuck—this time on a gravel bar—I offered to spell him dragging the raft. He wouldn't have it. I could see what he was thinking: I wouldn't be able to drag it very fast or very far. He had twenty pounds on me, and it was all muscle.

I kept looking for my first glimpse of the village. For the time being, only the crest of the Sierra del Carmen was showing above the tassels of the cane.

We came to a stretch where the water was pooled up for a good long run, and Rio was able to make some time. Along came a break in the giant cane lining the Mexican shore, and Boquillas suddenly appeared on its rocky bench above the river. Against the backdrop of purple-black clouds and lightning attacking the Sierra del Carmen, its squat adobe houses were wildly picturesque. Unfortunately, we were only halfway there.

Most of that second mile Rio splashed ahead of the raft, dragging it by a short length of rope. The turtles evacuated their basking rocks like a monster was approaching. It was unreal how hard Rio was working. Was this any way to run a river?

As for me, I only had to step into the river here and there. Dragging the canoe was easy, and it was never long before I got back in. As we finally drew close to the village, the sun had set. Rio wasn't concerned. Dusk lasts a long time in the middle of the summer, he pointed out. He redoubled his efforts, rowing hard against the wind.

The village was directly above us at last, on the right-hand side. From below, we could see only a couple of houses. Rio rammed the raft against the small beach at the foot of a trail down from the village. The raft held in the sand. I paddled in next to him. "My first time in Mexico!" I announced as I was about to step out.

"Stay in the canoe!" Rio ordered.

"How come?"

"You can stand in the river but not on the shore.

That's considered a visit to Boquillas, and Boquillas is off-limits."

"Say what? I thought we were going to visit the village."

"Did I say that? I said we were going to drop off the donations. That's all we're allowed to do."

"Says who?"

"Uncle Sam. After 9/11, the government closed the informal border crossings along the river. Part of the war on terror."

"Is Uncle Sam watching us right now?"

"Without doubt."

Rio took a quick look, then pointed across to the Texas shore, where a dirt track met the river at a break in the cane grass. A green-and-white Border Patrol truck was on its way down to the river. "See, they've got us spotted. He's going to park right across from us to make sure we mind our p's and q's. If we visit the village we're subject to a five-thousand-dollar fine."

"Ouch. That's beyond my budget. I've got a hundred dollars on me and a hundred I left at your place. Say, how will they know up in the village that we brought some stuff for them?"

Rio said that wouldn't be a problem. The black garbage bags on the front of the raft were our calling card. They could pretty well guess we were bringing scraps for making quilts, and other donations.

While we were waiting for the villagers in the gathering dusk, Rio filled me in on Boquillas. A hundred years before, it had sprung to life as a silver mining town. The ore went across the river on a bucket tram and was transported by mule-drawn wagons all the way to the railroad at Marathon, Texas. When the mines went bust, the town dwindled to a village and nearly emptied out. It came back to life after World War II with the creation of Big Bend National Park across the river. Boquillas was flourishing in the 1980s and '90s, with all the tourists visiting from across the river. They crossed in a small metal rowboat called the *Enchilada* and took a burro ride up to the village, where they bought meals and drinks and souvenirs. The people from Boquillas crossed to do their shopping at the store in Rio Grande Village.

Back in May 2002, everything suddenly changed. Overnight, the United States closed the border crossing. Before long, Boquillas was going bust again. The village was one of the most remote in all of Coahuila, which in turn was one of the most remote states in Mexico. The nearest shopping was 120 miles south on a bad dirt road, and the bus ran only one day a week. A couple dozen men had seasonal work fighting fires in the U.S., and another dozen had jobs at a lodge high in the Sierra del Carmen, but other than that, there wasn't work in Mexico to be had. From three hundred, the population of the village was down to less than a hundred.

Two Texas women, a former river guide from Terlingua and a woman from Marathon who used to teach in the Boquillas school, decided to try to help if they possibly could. They hit on the idea of teaching the women of the village to make quilts and founded a volunteer group called Fronteras Unlimited. The idea worked. The quilts were sold at galleries in Terlingua and at church auctions across West Texas. The money coming in from the quilts was making a big difference. For the time being, Boquillas was hanging on.

Dark was nearly upon us when we spied a couple dozen villagers, from kids to old people, starting down the path. Halfway down the hill, the Boquillans recognized Rio. They had big smiles on their faces as they closed in on us, everybody calling out, *"Hola, Rio!"* and *"Bienvenidos!"*

What blew me out of the water was how astoundingly fluent Rio was. I truly couldn't tell the difference between his Spanish and theirs. I wished I understood what they were saying. I had taken a little Spanish in school, but they spoke so fast I got only the gist of what they were talking about, and sometimes not that much. Rio asked if they had seen the helicopters. They had, but they didn't know what was going on. Rio asked after a woman named Señora Madrid. He was chagrined to find out she wasn't home. Señora Madrid was away. At least, that's what I thought they were saying.

Rio thanked them and told them we were in a hurry to get down the river and make camp while we could still see. They quickly unloaded the donations. In no time we were on our way again. Rio bent his back to the oars and yelled, *"Hasta pronto,"* to his friends. As I paddled downstream I found myself wondering why he had said, "See you soon."

I didn't give it a second thought. I was much more

interested in the Border Patrolman who'd been watching us from across the river. In the murky twilight, he turned his truck around and drove back up through the cane. Rio said he wouldn't be able to track us after this. He was at the end of the road.

Twenty minutes later, with bats flitting all around us, we were approaching the monumental entrance to Boquillas Canyon, a towering gate of solid stone, hugely impressive as a silhouette. Rio was promising a campsite barely inside the canyon.

He found the campsite, on a high sandbar on the Mexican side. Strange to say, it was okay with the U.S. if river runners camped in Mexico. They just couldn't stop at a village.

We put up the tent by the light of our headlamps. I asked if we should set up our kitchen next, and find something for supper. "Not for me," Rio said. "There's a path back to the village from here. I've got some business to take care of."

"What kind of business?"

"I'm carrying twenty-three hundred dollars from Ariel. It's a month's earnings from the quilt sales for the women of Boquillas. Ariel said I was supposed to give it to Señora Madrid, and her only. She's the one who distributes it, and she's away at a ranch."

"You sure you can't give it to somebody else to hold until she gets back?"

"Ariel didn't say. That's a huge amount of money for a village that poor. . . . I'm not going to take any chances.

Not to worry, Dylan. I'm going to hotfoot it back to Boquillas. Somebody with a truck is going to take me to Señora Madrid. She's at a ranch somewhere along the road south. She's the village midwife and went there to deliver a baby."

"How soon will you get back?"

"Middle of the night, maybe? I didn't catch how far away the ranch was. You just hang tight. Make yourself something to eat. Have a good night's sleep."

"Uh, I don't think so," I said. "I'm going with you."

A Little Side Trip into Mexico

THERE WAS JUST NO way I was going to wait there alone in the dark, on the Mexican shore no less, wondering when and if my cousin was going to return. We grabbed a couple of energy bars and a gallon jug of drinking water and took off.

With no streetlights and the village half abandoned, Boquillas was like Terlingua Ghost Town, only more so. You could tell the houses that were still occupied. With soft light from low-wattage bulbs seeping out through the windows, they glowed like candle lanterns. The village was eerily quiet until a dog detected our approaching footsteps and erupted with a full-throated alarm. A couple more dogs joined in. The hackles stood up on the back of my neck.

A door squeaked open. *"Quién es?"* a man called.

Rio identified himself. The man yelled at the dogs, and they quit barking. A few minutes later my cousin and I squeezed into the cab of a beat-up compact pickup, me in the middle, and headed down the dusty dirt road leading out of Boquillas. Fortino was the name of our white-maned driver. The old man didn't speak English, but he understood some. He nodded along as Rio told me that one of his sons was in Montana right now fighting a forest fire, and another was working up at the lodge in the nearby Sierra del Carmen.

Rio went on to tell me that Fortino was the one who used to ferry the tourists across the river in the *Enchilada* before the border was closed. Nowadays, Fortino made some money for his family and the village school by wading to the middle of the river below the Boquillas Canyon Overlook and serenading the tourists with songs of friendship and peace. They left the money in a can Fortino could reach without setting foot on the American shore.

The road was rough, and it felt like the old man's rattletrap didn't have shocks, same as it didn't have seat belts. I wondered if I was going to lose some fillings, or even my life. I wished Rio would ask him to slow down. The road was badly washboarded, and five minutes wouldn't go by without us going into a skid. Fortino was good at steering out of them—I'll give him that. After every skid he kept his speed down for half a minute maybe, then it was off to the races again. I pondered how incomprehensible it would be when my parents got a call from the U.S.

Embassy in Mexico: "We regret to inform you that your son Dylan has been killed in a rollover on a remote road in the Mexican state of Coahuila."

Some more chatter from Rio took my mind off my imminent demise. He told me he'd been down this road once before, on the weekly bus with Ariel on one of her missions across the river with Fronteras Unlimited. When the women of Boquillas had a bunch of new quilts to sell, one of the volunteers from Terlingua would cross the river to pick them up and take them back across.

To return to the American side, the volunteer had to cross at an official port of entry. The closest one was at Del Rio, Texas, a couple hundred miles downriver. Getting back to Terlingua from Boquillas entailed a journey of three days and nearly six hundred miles, beginning with a four-hour bus ride down the dirt road we were presently traveling. "I saw a lot of the emptiest part of Mexico," Rio told me. "It's rough country, and kind of scary."

You aren't telling me anything I don't already know, I thought. Just then Fortino rounded a corner and we came upon red and blue flashing lights, a roadblock in the middle of nowhere. The police were out of their vehicles and heavily armed. They were motioning for Fortino to stop, and they meant *now*. They raised their assault rifles, ready to mow us down if he didn't stop, and quick. "Policía Federal" was written large on the side of their vehicles, two cruisers and a tanklike truck.

Somehow Fortino managed to brake without losing control or getting us ventilated with bullets. *"Federales,"*

Rio muttered. "No worries, Dylan."

Huh? I was going to be lucky if I didn't mess my pants.

"Say as little as possible and don't make any sudden moves, okay?"

I was finding it difficult to speak. I couldn't even swallow. "Got it," I managed.

The federal police threw spotlights on us. The glare was blinding. Two of the black-uniformed policemen fanned out to cover us while a third approached Fortino's window, service pistol drawn. Fortino lowered his window. I noticed him placing both hands high on the steering wheel where they could be seen.

The policeman's face looked like it had been carved from the sharp, cruel stone of the surrounding desert. He pointed the flashlight at our faces and laps and down by our feet.

I began to breathe again, at least, when he holstered his weapon. He began to question Fortino. "*No se habla español,*" the old man said about us—they don't speak Spanish. I understood Fortino to say that we were on our way to catch up with a señora who was at a ranch delivering a baby. Stone Face bought that, but he wasn't buying the explanation for why Rio and I were along, whatever it was. He wagged his finger at the two of us. "*Identificación!*" he ordered. "ID!"

"Sorry," Rio said in English. "We don't have it with us. No ID." Which was true—it was back with our stuff on the raft.

A smile played at the policeman's lips. "You two get out. We find out your story at the station."

Uh-oh, I thought. This is going to be bad, real bad.

Stone Face left the window and walked back toward his cruiser to confer with his backup. The three *federales* huddled for a minute, maybe discussing which of them was going to take us in.

"*Mordida?*" Rio whispered to Fortino.

"*Sí,*" the old man replied.

"You just asked if they're going to mess us up?" I asked my cousin.

"I asked if we should try a bribe, and Fortino said yes."

"You've got that envelope full of money behind the seat."

"That much money is nothing but trouble. I pull that out, we get taken in for sure. Do you have that hundred on you that you were telling me about?"

"It's in my pants pocket."

Rio's eyes went to the policeman, who was on his way back. "Hurry—give it to Fortino."

Quick as I could, I fished it out and slipped it to Fortino, five folded twenties.

I understood next to nothing of the ensuing conversation between the old man and Stone Face. Obviously this had to be done delicately. The conversation ended when Fortino showed the money, and the policeman took it.

Stone Face scolded us about not carrying ID, and we were on our way. Another half hour, and we turned onto a side road, which was badly rutted. Just after midnight the road ended at the edge of nowhere, which would have been a good name for the ranch where we piled out.

The baby had been delivered within the hour. Right away, Rio gave the midwife the envelope from Ariel with the $2,300 in it. We would've made a quick turnaround, only Señora Madrid had some news to tell. Evidently it was a bombshell. The Spanish was flying so fast and furious, I never caught on. I got the idea that something really bad had happened nearby, and not very long ago.

As we got under way, lightning and thunder rent the night sky and bullets of rain pelted the windshield. Rio told me that Señora Madrid had been stopped at the same roadblock we were. The *federales* didn't hassle her. When she asked what the roadblock was for, they told her there'd been an incident at the lodge up in the Sierra del Carmen—a raid, and killings, and a kidnapping.

"You got my attention," I said. "Tell me everything you know."

A bolt of lightning struck directly ahead and lit up the surrounding desert. The dry wash we were about to cross was suddenly filling from the cloudburst. Fortino raced across it, splashing water high on both sides.

With Fortino's wipers going full speed and barely able to keep up, Rio began to fill me in. The lodge where the killings happened, he explained, was located inside a vast nature preserve in the high-elevation forest. The men from Boquillas who had jobs there either worked in the lodge itself or guided hunts for wild turkey, black bear, and elk.

Rio said that his father had been inside the lodge once, back when his dad was doing wildlife surveys for the preserve. "There's an airstrip up there," Rio said. "The lodge flies in groups from all over the world—have a mini-conference, bag an elk."

"Cut to the chase! What happened up at the lodge?"

"Here's what the police told Señora Madrid. Early yesterday morning, some men with automatic weapons burst into the lodge and killed some judges. Somebody was kidnapped as the killers were getting away. That's all Señora Madrid knew."

"What about the helicopters?"

"She said the *federales* didn't say anything about them. I'm guessing Mexico asked the U.S. to help in the manhunt."

"But why?"

"Maybe we could get there sooner—our closest army base is closer than theirs?"

"Sounds like the lodge didn't have enough security."

"They didn't think they needed much, on account of how isolated they are."

"Judges? Why judges?"

"All I can figure is, the judges who were meeting at the lodge were helping the government put the leaders of the drug cartels in jail. They must have been judges who weren't corrupt, who couldn't be bribed. One of the reasons the cartels have become so powerful is that they've been able to pay off government officials and law enforcement. The new president is fighting back. He's sent in the army to help local police. People are getting killed on both sides, something like three thousand already this year. Kidnapping has gotten out of hand, especially in Mexico City."

"Who's getting kidnapped?"

"Business executives, their family members, officials, sometimes tourists. Some of the ransoms are in the millions."

"Seems pretty spooky, this happening in the mountains right above us."

"It shouldn't affect us on the river. We just have to keep our eyes open, that's all."

The storm kept up all the way back to Boquillas. Three times, Fortino made it through flooded swales in the road, and once we had to get out and push. We were pumped by the prospect of having a lot more water in the river to work with. I thought of Roxanne, and my cousin saying that tarantulas moving indoors was a sign that the weather was coming.

It was three thirty AM and still raining, though not as hard, when we tromped into camp by the light of our headlamps. Before leaving, we had pulled the raft and the canoe onto high ground and tied them securely. On our return, we were thrilled to find them still tied but floating nicely on much higher water.

Bone weary and ready to drop, we crawled into the tent and slipped into our sleeping sheets. I asked Rio if he had learned his Spanish at school and he said he did, but outside of class. It was mostly what the kids spoke. I asked how many kids were in the high school. He let out a yawn. "Last count, forty-seven."

"I like the sound of the rain on the tent," I mused. "You think it will keep coming?"

No reply. He was dead asleep. Half a minute later, so was I.

The Wax Makers

WE WOULD HAVE SLEPT in, but the heat drove us out of the tent by eight. The river was up and running. The rain had run off the desert like it was an iron skillet.

By nine we were back on the water. Swallows by the hundreds knifed this way and that, working the river for bugs. A few miles down the river we passed under a formation called Lizard Rock. With a stretch of the imagination I was able to make out the two-hundred-foot iguana climbing the cliffs.

It was a good thing Rio wasn't going to have to drag the raft through Boquillas Canyon. The heat was blistering. It was so hot that the turtles wouldn't leave the water to bask on the rocks. From time to time they poked up their heads. It was easy enough to see how the temperatures made summer the off-season for river running.

I made sure to drink lots of water. My guide guaranteed smashing headaches if I didn't. To cool off, we swam alongside our boats every so often. Back on the boats we stayed comfortable as long as our clothes stayed wet.

The surface of the river was mirror calm, reflecting the cathedral-like walls of Boquillas Canyon. The aura of tranquility didn't last long. We heard the sound of an approaching helicopter, unbelievably loud in the confines of the canyon. Here it was, one of those Black Hawks, flying low with a gunner at the side door. He waved; apparently it wasn't us they were after. Before long the gunship had chopped its way out of sight downriver.

Needless to say, our mood pivoted in its wake. We had a lot to chew on that seemed more than a little ominous. Apparently the manhunt was still on, and we were inside the search area.

Forty minutes later the gunship returned, headed upstream, and forty minutes after that, here it came again, patrolling downstream. This time we were having lunch on the shore, on a rock shelf on the Mexican side. The Black Hawk slowed down, and it hovered above us. The gunner dropped a small sack of something just down the beach. He waved, we waved back, and they took off.

"What do you suppose it is?" I asked my cousin.

"No idea," he said, running to pick it up.

A message is what it was, weighted in a bag of pebbles. BEWARE OF SUSPICIOUS PERSONS, it said. CAMPING ON

I fetched the mile-by-mile guide for Boquillas Canyon from the canoe. From our present position, the Hallie Stillwell Bridge was twenty miles downstream. The army was figuring that the river downstream of the bridge was beyond the reach of anyone fleeing the scene of the crime in the Sierra del Carmen. Twenty more miles, and we could breathe easy.

I asked Rio if he thought the killers would head toward the river.

"Unlikely," he replied. "This direction, everything would be practically straight down, and rugged beyond belief. The safest way for them to ransom their victim would be from inside a Mexican city. If the army thought they were headed for the river, we would be seeing more than this one helicopter."

"I wonder what the getaway plan was."

"My guess is, they had a vehicle stashed a few miles away."

"In a vehicle, wouldn't they run into roadblocks like the one we ran into last night?"

"Not if they were quick enough, not if they had a small plane waiting not very far away. Remote ranches have airstrips, and so do abandoned mines. Who knows where they are by now."

"Something could have gone wrong with their plan. Maybe they bailed out on this side of the mountains, just running for their lives."

"I guess the army isn't ruling that out. That possibility would explain why the army assigned one of their Black Hawks to patrol the river, and why they warned us about 'suspicious persons.'"

We put back on the river, anxious to put the miles and the nerve-racking Black Hawk behind us. In the afternoon the clouds boiled up and dumped buckets of rain, which cooled things off and raised the river some more. We kept going.

After an hour the rain let up. The Black Hawk was back, and so was the heat. Overhead, vultures were circling. Our goal for the day was to float the entire length of Boquillas Canyon—sixteen miles. Tomorrow we would put the bridge behind us.

I had the guidebook in the canoe and kept referring to it. Ahead, a tower of stone with a peculiar top rose from the Texas side. For obvious reasons, the formation was called the *Oídos del Conejo*—Ears of the Rabbit. Opposite the Rabbit Ears was the last marked campsite in the canyon, but it was on the Mexican shore. Rio knew of an unmarked campsite on some ledges a few miles farther on, at the very end of the canyon. He knew this stretch like the back of his hand.

Half an hour later I was eager to call it a day, get out of the canoe, and ease my aching back. I kept scanning the Texas shore in search of those ledges Rio had talked about, but saw only cliffs and rockslides.

Rio wasn't looking left. His eyes were on the right, on the Mexican side.

I paddled close to the raft to see what he had in mind. "That ledges camp you're thinking about . . . it isn't on the Mexican side, is it?"

"No campsites on the Texas side," he replied tersely. "None on public land, anyway, that we could reach before dark. After the canyon, the river goes through a floodplain where the banks are solid cane, both sides. The camp I'm shooting for has some nifty sleeping shelters under an overhang, which will be handy if the weather comes up during the night. We'll be fine."

My cousin was feeling lucky about not running into any bad guys. Me, not so much. Side by side, we drifted on. The very end of the canyon came in sight. So did some people, on the ledges on the Mexican side. "Hey, Rio, there's some men down there."

"I see 'em. They're right where I wanted to camp."

We were out of the main current and drifting slowly. Another minute, and there was a lot more to see. Three men were working at a large metal vat erected over a fire pit that was open on the side facing the river. One of the men was stoking the fire while the other two, with long sticks, poked or stirred whatever they were boiling. Weeds, apparently: four huge mounds of bundled weeds lay close at hand. Some burros were grazing the grass at the edge of the cane.

The men stirring the vat suddenly noticed us. One dropped his stirring stick and ran along the bank, beckoning for us to come to shore. "Beware of suspicious persons," I reminded Rio.

"Those guys don't look suspicious," my cousin replied.

"Are you out of your mind? See those machetes at their waists? They look like *bandidos* out of central casting."

"I agree, but do they look like killers and kidnappers?"

"To me, I guess—yeah. I'll say yeah. They look exactly like killers and kidnappers."

Rio put the oar handles under his knees, leaned back and laughed. "You're way wrong. They look exactly like *candelilleros*."

"Candle-ee-AIR-os . . . ?"

"Wax makers. They're making wax from a weed called *candelilla*. This used to be a wax camp years ago . . . the wax plants have grown back, and they've come back to harvest them."

"Wax? Wax for what?"

"Candles, match heads, chewing gum—you name it."

By now we were within a hundred yards of the wax camp. The one trying to call us in was beckoning more urgently than ever. "They need help, or they want to talk," Rio said.

"Let's not and say we did," I pleaded.

"I guarantee you, Dylan. These are the nicest, most generous people you're ever going to meet."

"You mean, you know them?"

"Not personally."

Hmmm . . . , I thought.

Rio kept rowing toward the Mexicans. I couldn't believe it. My cousin waved and smiled as he drew close.

They caught his boat and held it against the shore. They were beside themselves saying thank you, and smiling, and adding more thank yous.

I hung back in the canoe, ready to back-paddle fast as I could.

Rio motioned me to come to shore.

I did, without taking my eyes off those machetes.

Now they had ahold of my boat, too. Their beards were unkempt and their clothes were badly soiled. On their gnarled feet they wore tire-tread sandals. "They lost their rowboat," Rio told me. "They think *mojados* took it—people trying to cross to the U.S. to find work."

"Did they see them take it?"

"No, they were asleep."

The wax makers wanted us to look for their rowboat— downstream, on the Texas side. They were pretty sure we would find it pulled up in the cane grass. Behind the cane, Rio told me, there was a dirt road that led to a paved road and eventually to Marathon. From Marathon the crossers could jump a train to either San Antonio or El Paso.

Rio promised them we would bring their rowboat back across if we found it. We said good-bye and angled across the river. On the way, Rio explained that without their rowboat, they wouldn't be able to sell their wax. They had a Texas buyer all lined up, but now they wouldn't be able to smuggle their product across.

"Smuggle? Those guys are smugglers?"

"Only as far as Mexico is concerned. It's illegal for them to take it out of the country. But they make more money if they can sell it across the border, so they do it whenever they can. It isn't illegal for the American buyers because the U.S. doesn't charge a duty on candelilla wax. Unlike those quilts from Boquillas, it doesn't have to go through customs."

"When they cross to our side, how come they don't get picked up as illegals?"

"They would if they got caught. Check out where we are. Nobody's looking."

On the Texas side, we hugged the shore, keeping our eyes peeled for their rowboat or the slightest indication of disturbance in the cane. We came up empty. The wax makers were going to have to sell their wax in Mexico, Rio said, or else wait a couple of months for the water to come down. By October, most years, they'd be able to wade this stretch of the river again.

The day was pretty well shot, and now we were passing through a wide, low valley—the floodplain Rio had talked about. Both shores were choked solid with a wall of the bamboo-like cane soaring up to twenty feet high and overhanging the water. Dusk was gathering and we were anxious to get off the river.

The only excuse for a campsite we could find, a couple of miles after we floated past the national park boundary, was on the Texas side. The guidebook had it marked as an old cattle ford. The place sure enough reeked of cattle, and it was littered with fresh pies. PRIVATE RANCH NO TRESPASSIN, the sign said. TRESPASSERS WILL BE SHOT ON SITE.

"Hmmm . . . ," I said. "What do you think, Rio?"

"It's public land again after a few more miles—Black Gap Wildlife Area—but we'd be nuts to float in the dark. Let's stay here, but not set up the kitchen, in case we need to beat a hasty retreat."

"From the landowner?"

"Or his heat-packing hired hands, or an aggressive bull. If we have to get back on the river we will."

The wind was stirring and a thunderstorm was brewing. We ate a can of tuna apiece and then we pitched the tent.

The stars stayed out, no cattle appeared, and neither did cowboys packing heat. We woke to day three and an incredible view of the Sierra del Carmen upriver. It was a huge relief to have put those mountains behind us.

We wondered if the manhunt was still on, but we didn't have to wonder long. We were eating breakfast on the boats—Raisin Bran with rice milk—when the Black Hawk flew by. Within minutes it was headed back upriver.

No new messages.

The Point of No Return

PERCHED ON A BLUFF on the Mexican side, the abandoned village of La Linda appeared as we rounded a bend. Its whitewashed church with twin bell towers looked sadly beautiful against a backdrop of stony hills. We had the Hallie Stillwell Bridge in our sights. Beyond the bridge, no more Black Hawks. We'd be good to run the river without fear.

We floated under the bridge, a real eyesore. Concrete barriers, chain link, and razor wire made it impossible for pedestrians as well as vehicles to cross. Even so, a man in a green-and-white pickup—Border Patrol—was keeping watch from the American side. Just past the bridge, where the river made a sharp left, an abandoned chemical plant appeared on the Mexican side. The bridge had been built for trucks to haul a chemical called fluorspar sixty miles north to the railroad.

Rio pointed to a bulldozed swath of the riverbank on the Texas side. "This is where we would've launched for the Lower Canyons if we hadn't added on the extra mileage for Ariel."

"It turned out to be kind of high anxiety, but I'm glad we did."

"It's time to start with the new guidebook. Let's go to shore and pull it out."

We beached our boats, got out and stretched our legs, and chewed on some jerky. Rio fished the guidebook for the Lower Canyons out of his waterproof day bag. "So, Dylan, you wanna take a look?"

"You bet. I barely glanced at it back in Terlingua."

I took a seat on the raft and turned to the introduction. Suddenly I had a lot more to chew on than beef jerky. Here's what it said:

Without doubt the Lower Canyons section of the Rio Grande, with its spectacular scenery, whitewater, and rugged wilderness character, makes for one of the great river adventures in North America. Anyone considering this section must factor in the combination of its length—83 miles—with its extreme remoteness. It is in fact the most rugged and remote section of the entire 2,000-mile border between the United States and Mexico. Preparations need to be exhaustive. Exercise caution at all times, on and off the river. If you injure

yourself or damage essential gear beyond repair,
help is not on the way. You may well not see
another human being during the duration of your
trip. Hiking out through the desert can be fatal,
especially during the summer.

Soon as I finished that opening paragraph, I read it a second time. I would be lying if I didn't admit that it gave me the jitters. What would we do if we broke a leg? What if one of us got appendicitis or got bit by a snake?

Downstream from here, we were going to be way out on a limb, and if something happened, we couldn't call for help.

Did Rio have a satellite phone along, and just didn't tell me?

What were the chances? He didn't have a phone of any description at home, and sat phones are expensive, even to rent.

Here you are, I told myself, about to take your last step on the slippery slope. Think, you fool. Stop and think.

I tried to appear casual as I reached for my water bottle and took a long drink. Rio was skipping stones on the river. He wasn't in a rush; just the opposite. He had called for this break, at this exact spot, because it was the point of no return.

I turned to the first map. It showed the put-in where we were standing. It showed the bridge. On the Mexican side was La Linda. On the American side was a ranch, Heath Canyon Ranch. The map showed a paved road leading north to Marathon. Somewhere along that road was a turnoff for Big Bend National Park and Terlingua. If we decided to bail out here, we could get the Border Patrolman to radio Terlingua. If that didn't work out, we could walk to the ranch. We could ask them to call Terlingua for us, call Ariel.

What about Hurricane Dolly? The Border Patrolman watching the bridge would know what the hurricane was up to. Had it made landfall in east Texas or Louisiana, like they thought it would? What if, against the odds, it had come ashore at the mouth of the Rio Grande and was heading for the Lower Canyons this minute? Shouldn't we at least be asking?

The Border Patrolman wouldn't be able to tell us for sure if we were going to run into Dolly. The storm could veer any which way. He could only give us the latest odds.

Should I bring it up with Rio?

If I did, would he entertain the idea of quitting on the trip just because we might run into rough weather? Not hardly. He'd been picturing high water from the start. It was why he'd brought the raft along.

Stop, I told myself. Just stop. You've got your mind chasing its tail. The first thirty-three miles were only to drop the donations off at Boquillas. All the whitewater is downstream. Just quit worrying and do what you came all this way to do.

Rio was no longer skipping stones. I closed the mile-by-mile guide and spit out a wad of jerky gristle. "You still on Mile 1?" he said. "Reading all about La Linda and the DuPont plant?"

75

"Just thinking. I've been doing too much thinking, actually."

"About whether we should commit, now that we're here?"

"Yeah, sure."

"I saw you reading the introduction—the big heads-up."

"They don't pull any punches."

"One thing I forgot to mention back home—I've never been past here."

He'd said it casually, but this was big. "You mean, downstream of the bridge?"

"Yeah, right."

"You mean you haven't run the Lower Canyons before?"

"Never laid eyes on it, except in pictures."

"But I thought you'd done it with your dad."

"I never said that, did I?"

"I just assumed, I guess."

"My dad hasn't run it for the last two years. None of the guides have. There isn't much market for week-long trips. Some private river runners do it, mostly in the spring."

"Man, that's different."

"Different from what?"

"From what I was thinking."

"Okay, it's different, and maybe I should've told you, but would it have made any difference?"

"I don't know . . . I could have factored it in . . . I guess not."

"So, you're good with it? We can always go home and shoot hoops, watch DVDs of *Man vs. Wild*. Hey, no pressure. I'm cool with whatever you decide."

I hesitated. The heat was so intense, it was hard to think at all. *This is it*, I told myself.

No doubt Rio could hear my gears grinding. Here's what I kept coming back to: You play it safe, you'll disappoint your cousin and yourself. You'll have to live with that.

"I'm in," I told him. "I'm going all the way, till the wheels fall off and burn."

"That's what I was hoping to hear, *mi primo loco*."

Rio had just called me his crazy cousin. This felt great, absolutely great. We slapped hands and got back on the river.

Floating under the walls of Heath Canyon and then Temple Canyon—tantalizing appetizers of the mighty Lower Canyons to come—we passed into the broken and rugged country beyond. Once again the quiet of the wilderness prevailed. We were beyond the reach of the helicopter patrol; we'd left all that madness behind.

Everything on the Texas side was part of the Black Gap Wildlife Area, and we were seeing wildlife. We watched a herd of bighorn sheep, their young included, charge down a slope that would've made an extreme skier vomit. They were doing all sorts of insane aerials, huge leaps off of boulders, just unbelievable stuff. We thought for sure a mountain lion must be chasing them, but it turned out nothing was. They were simply having fun on their way down to get a drink.

We floated past a huge rock formation on the Mexican side called *El Caracol*—The Snail—and ran the Class 2 rapid below a dry wash on the Texas side. The bow of my canoe caught some air, but I took on barely enough water to soak my boat sponge. The best part was, Rio liked my style. He could see I was far from being a novice.

Downstream we found a shady beach, went swimming, and took naps. We were living the life of Huck Finn. I had made the right call.

At Mile 13 we replenished our freshwater jugs from the springs that emerged between rock layers on the Texas side. We were lucky the river wasn't any higher, or the springs would have been underwater.

We made it all the way to *Las Vegas de los Ladrones*, the Outlaw Flats, at Mile 17. A grassy flat on the Mexican side in front of a spectacular butte called *El Sombrero* made for a perfect campsite. The grass had been mowed by cattle and all the pies were dry. The guidebook said we would be seeing quite a few cattle, "more than half wild."

We pitched the tent and set up our camp table and chairs. Rio dug out his fishing tackle, which wasn't the kind I was expecting. It consisted of a tackle box and a couple of laundry detergent jugs, capped and empty. I'd never done any jug fishing but I'd heard of it. The basic idea is to suspend a couple of hooks from the jug, which serves as a float. For anchors, Rio had brought along four-inch lengths of heavy construction rebar.

We put together two juglines with two leaders apiece.

At the end of each leader we tied on a hook.

For bait, Rio had brought along a block of Zote Soap. That, I'd never heard of. "Made in Mexico," I read aloud. "Sixty-six percent animal fat. Zote Soap is safe for the environment and safe for your family."

"Not to mention, catfish go crazy over it," Rio added. "The citronella scent is what does it." He sliced off four chunks and baited the hooks. "We'll try Spam if the soap doesn't do the trick."

We deployed the juglines in the pool just down from our campsite. One of them produced a yellow catfish, a ten pounder. Rio carved two fillets and fried them up. As the sun was setting and the full moon was rising over that big wide-open country, we feasted. Ten more miles and we would be inside the Lower Canyons.

I slept well on a belly full of catfish, and woke to clear skies. By the time we were pouring pancake batter on the griddle, things were changing. A skirmish line of clouds was heading our way from downstream. Rio remarked that it was early in the day for thunderstorms to be cooking. This looked more like a front.

"Front?" I repeated. "Front, as in tropical storm front?"

"Possibly. Our garden-variety thunderstorms boil up out of the clear blue sky. This is something else."

"Can't be Dolly," I said after some thought.

"Why not, Dylan?"

"This front is coming from downstream. The map shows us running north and a little east until the last fifteen miles of our trip. The Gulf of Mexico is south and east."

Rio shook his head. "Nice try! Tropical storms have a counterclockwise spin. The first band would arrive from the northeast."

"Hmmm . . . ," I said. "That might be exciting."

"Something to tell my dad about. He'd be sick that he missed it."

Just then came the sound of a snapping twig from the brush at the back of the campsite. We heard shuffling feet. We spun around on our chairs. Scarcely twenty feet away, a man and a boy stood at the edge of the clearing. I about jumped out of my skin. What were they doing here, in the absolute middle of nowhere?

"Don't be alarmed, my friends," the man said in heavily accented English, raising his hand in a peaceful gesture.

Their clothes were torn, and their faces, hands, and arms were badly scratched. They looked like they hadn't slept for a week.

"We lost our way . . . had a rough time . . . need some help," the man said. About forty, he was wearing jeans and a short-sleeved shirt—white polyester. The boy was my little brother's age, right around seven. He was wearing a soccer jersey. Underneath the name of the team, LIVERPOOL FOOTBALL CLUB, were the words *You'll Never Walk Alone.*

The man had a beard of sorts, a week's growth of coarse black stubble. The scar dead center on his forehead, mostly above his hairline, made you want to look away. His eyes were all over the place, assessing us and our gear—the kitchen, the tent, the boats.

The boy had yet to look at us. His eyes were on the ground. One eye was blackened, and the cheek on the same side was bruised. He was covered with cuts and scratches. As my own hands would testify, nearly every plant in the desert had its way to draw blood, and it looked like the boy had stumbled or fallen into more than a few. The man kept one hand clamped on his shoulder.

Evidently they weren't related. They weren't acting like it, and their faces didn't bear a family resemblance.

"Are you hungry?" Rio asked. "How about some breakfast?"

"Please," the man replied. "We haven't eaten in days."

The man and the boy approached us. The man had a small backpack that he placed under our table, next to the gas bottle. "I am Carlos," he said. "The boy is Diego. Do you speak Spanish?"

Rio hesitated. "Not that much," he said, which surprised me. "Keep speaking English," he went on, "so my cousin can understand. I'm Rio, he's Dylan. Come, sit down on these chairs. We'll make more pancakes, and we could also fry up some meat, if you don't mind Spam."

The Mexican flashed a wide smile. "Like they say in the U.S.A., beggars can't be choosers."

The Coyote's Story

CROSSERS," RIO WHISPERED AS we worked side by side at the table mixing more pancake batter and slicing Spam.

"They're in really bad shape," I whispered back, "especially the boy."

Carlos was watching us over his shoulder from the chair alongside Diego's. He seemed suspicious of our whispers. The Mexican was stocky, with a wrestler's build—not somebody you would want to tangle with. I didn't know what it was about him that made me so uneasy.

"We can spare them some food," Rio whispered.

"We're in a lot better shape than they are," I agreed. "We have to help."

"What you guys talking about?" Carlos called.

"Our food supply," Rio said. "We're kind of on short rations. Not to worry, we're making you a meal that will fill you up."

Pretty quick, we brought them plates heaped with pancakes and fried Spam. Carlos accepted a knife and fork, and said yes to maple syrup. "Diego," I said as I handed the boy his plate, "would you like syrup on your pancakes?"

I made a pouring motion with the syrup. He nodded without looking me in the eye.

The boy ate ravenously, with his hands, like a starving raccoon. I filled a liter bottle from one of our five-gallon water jugs and set it by his foot. He drank half immediately. A minute later he drank the other half. "Diego," I asked as I refilled the bottle, "do you speak English?"

No response. It seemed like there was something seriously off about him.

Carlos gave the boy a scornful look. "I barely get his own language out of him. A spoiled brat is what he is. He don't deserve what his family is trying to do for him."

"Are you family, Carlos?" Rio asked. "His uncle, something like that?"

"Me, no, no way. I'm just doing my job. His mother in Chicago hired me to go to Mexico and bring him to her."

"Is that where you're from—Chicago?"

"*Sí, sí.* I live in Chi-ca-go for many years. This is what I do for a living. People go north without their children, and after a while, they pay someone to bring them across."

"So, you are a coyote."

"The good kind, not the kind you hear about, the ones that leave women and children in the desert to die. I'm not like them. This boy would rather stay with his grandmother in Mexico. He is afraid of his mother's boyfriend. He is afraid of the desert. He is afraid of everything. I've had it up to here with him."

"You got lost, you said?"

"*Sí*, we been wandering around for days. We had some food, but it was stolen."

"Where did you start from?"

"A town called Melchor Múzquiz. We followed dirt roads, but many times you could go this way or that way—no signs. For a long time now, no road at all. We were supposed to find a bridge across the river."

"You took a wrong turn all right. The only bridge in a stretch of hundreds of miles is seventeen miles upstream from here. Whoever told you that you could cross on it was mistaken. The bridge is sealed off, and the Border Patrol is always keeping watch there."

"You live in Texas?"

"Yes, in Terlingua, a hundred miles upstream and ten miles from the river. My cousin is visiting—first time in Texas."

"You two boys, you do this alone?"

"Yep, ten days, just the two of us."

"That's pretty crazy, no? This is wild country."

"That's what makes it fun."

"Fun," Carlos repeated with a wry grin. "The things

Americans do for fun—it's *loco*."

Rio gave him a big smile, and proceeded, casual and off-handed. "Tell me, Carlos . . . not very many people without documents try to cross in the Big Bend . . . Why are you crossing here instead of downstream in the valley, or upstream near El Paso? Or maybe Arizona?"

"I used those places before, and California. Your government is making it harder and harder. Where there is no wall, there are cameras and so many *Migra*—"

"Border Patrol," Rio translated.

"—thousands more *Migra* than there were even a year ago. You mark my words, many more people will try to cross in the Big Bend, even with the cliffs. If they have to try the roughest places, that's what they will do."

"We can give you a little food," Rio said. "What else can we do for you?"

Carlos ran his hand over the stubble on his chin and up the side of his face. "If the boy was in better shape, you could take us across the river, but the highway and the railroad are not close—am I right?"

"Sixty or seventy miles north."

"I could never drag this kid that far without killing him. His mother wouldn't appreciate that, eh, Diego?"

The boy was done eating and was licking his fingers. He didn't acknowledge that he'd been spoken to.

"Bad attitude," Carlos sneered. "Look, *amigos*, even my maps were stolen. If I could look at yours, I could figure out what to do next."

"No problem," Rio said, "but it only shows the river

and about fifteen miles on either side." He went to the raft to fetch the guidebook.

Carlos turned to me. "The weather is changing."

"Maybe a tropical storm," I said. "We heard that a hurricane was heading for the Gulf Coast of Texas. Maybe it already came ashore."

Carlos looked at the clouds racing in. They were about to blot out the sun. "You think this is it?"

"We hope not, but maybe it is."

Rio returned to the table, closed the lid of the Coleman stove, and placed the guidebook on it. He opened it to the first map, and Carlos stepped close. Rio pointed out the Hallie Stillwell Bridge and the roads—the dirt one heading south to Melchor Múzquiz and the paved one north to Marathon.

I sat down next to the boy. Diego had his head down, and was attempting to pull something from the back of one hand with his fingernails. I leaned over to see what it was. A tiny cactus needle. Now that I looked, I saw them all over his hands and his forearms. "Do those hurt?" I whispered.

He grimaced. I took that for a yes. Diego's lips were badly chapped. I offered my spare lip balm and he took it. I went to the raft and returned with the first aid kit. The cut on his head was infected, and some of his scratches soon would be if they weren't already.

As Rio and Carlos talked about the map, I swabbed the cut with alcohol wipes. Diego winced but appeared grateful. I applied antibiotic ointment and a square Band-

Aid that looked like it was going to stay put. Catclaw mesquite or something similar accounted for the cut and the scratches, but I was suspicious about the black eye and the bruised cheek.

Only with tweezers was I was able to pull the tiny cactus needles from Diego's hands and arms. It was a laborious process; there were hundreds of them. "I like your soccer jersey," I whispered as I worked. "Do you like soccer, Diego?"

He nodded mournfully. He knew the word *soccer*, as I'd guessed. Evidently he understood English; he might even be able to speak it. Why he wouldn't was painfully obvious. He was afraid. He'd been ordered to play dumb.

"Here we are at Mile 17," Rio was saying to the coyote. "Look, no roads on the Mexican side, but across the river, in the wildlife area, there's a four-wheel-drive road. If you followed that north and west, it would eventually lead you to the paved road to Marathon. With food, you could do it, not that I'm recommending it."

Carlos frowned. "Find me the next road down the river that goes south into Mexico."

"You're going to go back and try again?"

"I'm going to quit on this job—take the brat back to his grandmother in Torreón."

"Okay, let's take a look."

Rio and Carlos studied the maps and read the text on the opposite pages. The country was so wild and so rugged, they found no roads close to our present position, none on the Mexican side until San Rosendo Canyon, between

Miles 40 and 41. Rio read the text about the primitive hot springs pools at the river there and a rough road leading twelve miles up San Rosendo Canyon to a ranch. The ranch was described as "one of the most remote in all of Mexico."

"Only twenty-three miles from here to San Rosendo Canyon," Carlos said.

"True, but thirteen of those are in a canyon that's more than a thousand feet deep. You couldn't walk to San Rosendo Canyon from here. It would be easier to walk the seventeen miles from here upstream to the bridge. From there you could walk on the road south to Múzquiz."

"That would take a week!"

"I guess it might. If it rains, and it looks like it will, you'll find water. Do you want us to take you across the river instead, and try your luck walking to Marathon?"

"The boy would never make it. Take us on your raft to San Rosendo Canyon. Then we walk only twelve miles to that ranch to get help. They can drive us to town next time they go."

Rio hesitated, which surprised me. I was expecting him to agree. "Sorry, *señor*," he said. "I can't be responsible. We have three life jackets counting our spare, and none will fit Diego. If the tropical storm hits us, and it looks like it's going to, it might get really rough on the river."

"Between here and this San Rosendo Canyon—I see this on the map— there are only two rapids, both Class 1. That sounds like the easiest, no?"

"That may be true—the big stuff starts with the rapid at San Rosendo Canyon—but all the same, I can't be responsible. My cousin and I are on our own trip. Besides, you don't know that there's anybody home at that ranch twelve miles from the river. They might be there only part of the year, when they come to round up cattle."

The Mexican's forehead wrinkled around that angry scar. "You would abandon us?"

"We'll give you canned food and we'll even give you our tent. But no, I'm sorry, we can't take you along."

I had pulled as many cactus needles from Diego as I could. Some were too tiny for the tweezers to grab hold of. I used cotton balls and peroxide to clean up his face, arms, and hands. Both wrists had welts on them. When I finished, a tear dropped from his eye.

Rio and I packed quickly. We gave the man our canned meat and soup, a can opener, and a lighter. We gave them two milk jugs filled with clean water. And we gave them our tent.

We'd probably just saved their lives, but Carlos was far from grateful. His face was frozen with a scowl as we shoved off. The coyote looked like he wanted to murder us. The boy was streaming tears.

Flossing with Cane

THE WIND BEGAN TO blow, and blow hard. As much as I wanted to talk to Rio about what had just happened, we had to row and paddle hard to keep from being blown upstream. The clouds were swirling and thickening by the minute. We went to shore at a small beach to put away our sunglasses and pull on our rain gear. I asked Rio what he thought of Carlos, if that's what the coyote's name really was. "Spookiest guy I ever met," Rio said.

Rio suspected, same as me, that it was Carlos who had blackened Diego's eye and bruised his face. The welts on the boy's wrist, we figured, were from the man's belt used as a leash. We could only hope that the coyote would return him to his grandmother.

As it was, we would never know Diego's fate. It was all part of living on the border, Rio said. Every hour of every day there were desperate people moving through the desert. Most paid dearly to be guided by coyotes, who were quick to abandon them. Crossers were found dead every year. They died of heatstroke and hypothermia, of sickness and starvation. Some who survived, and some who didn't, had been beaten and abused.

"Maybe we could have taken Diego with us," I said, "and somehow got him back to his grandmother."

Rio shook his head emphatically. "That would have meant taking Carlos along, at least as far as San Rosendo Canyon. Having that scumbag in my raft—that would give me the creeps."

"Carlos should be grateful," I said with an eye on the weather. "He even has our tent."

"I only gave it to him on account of Diego."

"I know, and I'm glad you did."

"We'll get by, but we need to be on the hunt for shelter, a rock overhang or something."

Just then lightning began to fire, and the surrounding mountains rumbled with thunder. Downriver, the wind was blowing up whitecaps. I told Rio it was time to fish out the spray cover for the canoe before we went any farther.

"Looks like you're going to need it," he agreed. "A canoe makes a lousy submarine."

We transferred most of the heavy stuff I was carrying over to the raft, including two of our three five-gallon water jugs. After making sure that the rest of my storage was tied into the thwarts spanning the canoe, we pulled the canoe's spray cover out of its stuff bag. There were two separate pieces, the larger to cover the front half of the canoe and the smaller to cover the open space behind me. The seat and kneeling area, back of center, remained open to incoming waves, but it was the least likely location to take on water.

It was easy enough to spread the waterproof material over the gunwales, and to run the shock cord around the knobs on the outside of the hull. I made sure I had my bailer, boat sponge, and throw-bag handy. The spare paddle, too.

The clouds grew increasingly dark. Heavy rain wasn't far off. The question now became . . . wait this out or stay on the river? We had a quick huddle and decided we should put some miles behind us in case this got truly serious.

We were ready for battle, and as we put back on the water, we had one on our hands. Rio had to pull hard against the wind to get into the current. The sky broke open with a deafening thunderclap, and a squall line of low clouds hit us with gusts of wind and sheets of rain. I got off the canoe seat and for the first time on the trip assumed the more stable kneeling position, knees spread wide. I've always liked wild weather and it looked like I was going to see some.

The rain kept coming. Another mile downstream, and we were approaching a large island. As always, Rio was out front with the raft, by far more stable than the canoe. It was up to him to pick the best channel for us to take around the island.

As he drifted closer, Rio stood up on his rowing seat to get a better look at his choices. I was guessing he was going to pick the channel around the right side of the island. There was much more water going that direction. Generally, the more water, the fewer rocks you have to dodge.

Rio sat back down and rowed toward the right channel. I followed him in, keeping enough space between us to allow for the faster drift of the canoe. In a tight channel we would have a real problem if I jammed him and he lost the use of an oar.

As I rounded a corner and was able to see farther downstream, I saw Rio beating the river to froth as he tried to avoid a nasty hazard along the shore. The cane there, thick as a bamboo forest, was bending far into the river, right down to the waterline. As hard as Rio was rowing, it didn't look like he was going to be able to keep the raft from running headlong into it. The current was pulling him full bore into the overhanging cane.

I had to bear down. I would capsize for sure if the current swept me under the cane.

As I paddled toward the ribbon of safe water between the shore of the island and the powerful current surging into the cane, I glanced to the right through the pouring rain. Rio's raft ran smack into the overhanging wall of cane grass. At the moment his hands flew up to protect his face, he got broomed overboard.

Focus, I told myself. This is bad, really bad.

By now I was passing the raft by. It had been arrested in place, with only its stern showing and no sign of Rio. I failed to catch even a glimpse of his orange life jacket. I could only guess that he was hidden under the cane.

Our best shot, I figured, was for me to get downstream and catch him when he got flushed out. I raced another fifty yards to the foot of the island and paddled into the eddy on the right-hand side. The eddy water rushing upstream allowed me to hold my position below the downstream end of the overhanging cane. Still no Rio.

His straw hat floated by. I reached out and grabbed it.

I held my breath, fearing the worst. Finally, finally, the cane spit him out, just upstream from where I was waiting. His face had taken a thrashing.

My cousin was mighty happy to spot me, and vice versa. No need for the throw-rope. I intercepted him at the head of the eddy. He latched on to the grab-loop on the stern of the canoe and I towed him to the foot of the gravelly island.

Rio crawled out of the water all pumped up, running in place in the pouring rain. Not to keep warm; the river water wasn't cold and neither was the rain. Just to burn off the excess adrenaline, I figured.

"Bad situation back there," I said.

"I did it on purpose," he shot back.

This was too preposterous to be believed. "Oh yeah," I said, "what for?"

He bared his teeth. "I needed a good flossing, and I got one!"

I had a good laugh, and Rio admitted how embarrassed he was. He said he was "too slow on the draw," which was true. If he had cocked the raft toward the cane and pulled hard to the left a few seconds earlier, he would have escaped the current.

I asked if he had ever capsized a canoe in overhanging cane. He held up three fingers. I asked if he thought the cane would let the raft go, and he said he figured it would, thanks to the rain. With a little more power behind it, the current would rip it loose.

An hour later, the raft was still in the grasp of the cane. We waited some more, and we lucked out. The rising river tore the raft loose, none the worse for the thrashing but strewn with cane.

We're in the Big-Time Now

WE MADE IT ANOTHER eight miles on rapidly rising water to a possible shelter pictured in the Lower Canyons guidebook. Twenty-seven miles below the put-in at the bridge, a rock house stood back from the river on the Texas side, maybe fifty feet above the elevation of the river. The one-room structure was a remnant of an old candelilla works, the mile-by-mile guide said. A nearby spring provided an optimum water supply, always clear and clean, for rendering the wax.

Before we walked up the slope to check out the rock house, we located the spring and filled our water jugs to the brim. From here on, the springs might be flooded out.

On our way up to the rock house we caught a good view of the scaly mountains on the Mexican side. Their tops were shrouded in clouds. We climbed a little higher and saw that our rock house lacked a roof. That was okay, we figured—our big blue tarp could do the job.

It didn't work out. The inside of the building was choked with giant prickly pear cactus, their pads big as frying pans. The needles in the pads were as long as my little finger. Rio informed me that the pads were edible, if prepared correctly. "Uh, some other time," I told him.

Two miles downriver, at Mile 29, we found a place to camp on the Texas side. The large grassy sandbar there stood ten feet above the river and looked like a safe bet. While we were unloading the boats, however, the river came up another six inches. If it rose another nine and a half feet and flooded the campsite, we would be out of luck. Behind the sandbar, the cactus- and ocotillo-studded slope was as steep as a playground slide.

We liked our chances. Rio had never seen the river rise nine feet overnight. Unless we were very unlucky we would be okay, but what were we going to do for a shelter?

Rio wasn't worried. "No problem," he said. "Let's make like Comanches, and build ourselves a wickiup out of cane."

"Ever built one before?"

"No, but I've seen pictures."

Amid lightning and thunder and a new squall with pelting rain, we gathered cane. Our rescue knives borrowed from our life jackets went through the stalks like butter. "Ever seen this much water in the river?" I asked.

"It usually gets this high every summer."

"So, you don't think this is Dolly we're looking at?"

"It could be just a West Texas toad strangler. My dad and I have had the raft out a couple of times on five thousand cubic feet per second. We aren't looking at that much yet, but we're getting close."

"What's the biggest flow you've ever heard of?"

"At the takeout below Santa Elena Canyon, on the outside of one of the johns, the Park Service painted a black stripe to show the high-water mark from the summer of 1958. The mark is higher than the door."

"How much water was it?"

A huge grin spread across his face. "Fifty-two thousand."

Mindful of the wind, we made our shelter low to the ground, beginning with four forked sticks jammed waist high into the sand at the corners of a five-by-seven-foot rectangle. We laid sturdy cane stalks into the forks, framed the roof and the leaning walls with more stalks, spread our blue tarp over the frame, then covered the whole thing with layer upon layer of the grassy tops of the cane. We had ourselves a wickiup, with only a crawl hole open to the weather.

By five PM it was prematurely dark under the dense, black clouds. The lightning and thunder had backed off, but the rain kept coming. We inflated our ground pads and crawled into the shelter with a can of beans and an energy bar apiece, our second and last meal for the day.

It was snug in our shelter—not bad at all—and we got to talking. Rio asked me about a canoe stroke I'd been using, and where I learned it. I told him it was called the Canadian. They taught it at the canoe camp I had done twice with the Nantahala Outdoor Center. I waxed enthusiastic about the Nantahala River and its rapids, about the Great Smoky Mountains and the Blue Ridge and the town of Asheville. He said he would love to run a mountain river with forests right down to the water, and I said we had to make it happen one day.

By now it was nearly dark, and it had been raining all this while. We thought we'd better check on the boats, and it's a good thing we did. The river was already lapping at the base of the salt cedars they were tied to. We carried the canoe up the slope and out of harm's way, and used our seventy-five-foot rope to tie the raft to a boulder on the slope above.

On our way back to the shelter we came across two rattlesnakes displaced by the rising water. Scorpions, more than I cared to count, were scuttling for higher ground.

We reentered our shelter with extreme caution. Rio gave me a little advice: "If you feel a scorp on your face or whatever, don't grab it, just flick it off. They can sting you real quick."

We stayed up late playing cards by the light of our headlamps. We played every game for two that we knew—War, Crazy Eights, Go Fish, and Rummy.

My cousin fell asleep as soon as he put his head down. If it wasn't for my fear of scorpions, maybe I could've done the same. I kept feeling them on my face, on my hands, all over. I kept slapping them off. Were they real or imagined?

I was too warm, that's why I couldn't go to sleep. Our wickiup felt more like a Comanche sauna. I threw open the sleeping sheet but that didn't seem to help.

Time dragged as my mind raced to the tune of the muffled yet relentless rain. I kept thinking how far from home I was, and how far out on a limb. Knock it off, I told myself. It's gotta be way after midnight. Just knock it off. You're not in any real danger. The river sounds loud and scary in the dark, that's all.

I was nearly asleep—finally—when I had an eerie sensation. I was lying on my side, facing my cousin, when I felt something moving along my back, something distinctly snakelike.

Was I imagining it?

No way. The contraction of snake muscle along my spine was terribly real. I had a serious problem.

I tensed, and when I did, the snake stopped moving. What was the most common snake along the river corridor?

Rattlesnake, Rio had said.

What was the second-most common?

Copperhead.

I wanted to jump out of my skin. I wanted to scream. *Don't*, I told myself. Just chill. And hope it doesn't crawl across your face.

I realized I was holding my breath. I couldn't do that forever. I let it out slowly, took another, tried to breathe normally. All the while, my heart was going like a bass drum.

The snake was on the move again, tight against my T-shirt. Its head was following the contours of my back, and now my neck. It took forever for its body to follow in wavelike contractions of muscle.

When I thought it might be gone I rolled slightly toward Rio. In response, the snake rattled. I felt the vibration against my shoulder blade.

"Rattlesnake!" Rio whispered.

"Tell me about it. It's right behind me."

"Don't move."

"I won't."

Maybe five minutes later Rio whispered, "Is it still there?"

"No idea."

An eternity later, I still couldn't tell if it was gone. This might've been stupid, but I had to know. Slowly and cautiously, I reached for the spot where I had set my headlamp. To my great relief, my fingers came to rest on the headlamp and not a snake. I flicked it on, got up on one elbow, and shined it all around. "Can't see it," I reported, "but maybe it crawled around behind you."

"Well, look behind me!"

I got up on my knees and made a more thorough search. "I don't see it, Rio. It must've crawled back out, unless it's inside your sheet."

"Hey, that isn't funny."

"I know."

"You know what, the river must've kept rising. It sounds kind of close."

Uh-oh, I thought, and pointed the beam through our crawl hole.

"It *is* kind of close," I reported. "It's three feet from our door."

Lingering only long enough to pull on our rain gear and shoes and to stuff our sleeping sheets in our river bags, we bailed out of there. Five minutes later and we would've been sleeping with the fishes. We pulled the tarp free of our shelter's roof and scrambled up the slope with it and our ground pads, slipping and sliding and falling in the mud. We draped the tarp over a boulder, weighted it all around, and crawled underneath. There wasn't enough room to lie down, just a place to huddle, hemmed in by bristling cactus. What can I say; it was a long night.

Dawn came slowly, under a leaden sky and a steady rain. There wasn't a trace of our Comanche wickiup to be seen. It was on its way to the Gulf of Mexico. The high sandbar we had camped on was entirely underwater. The river was in flood, a turgid yellow-brown, swollen by the runoff from thousands of washes draining hundreds, maybe even thousands of square miles of desert. "We're in the big-time now," my cousin said.

Hello, Dolly

WE MIXED SOME POWDERED milk and ate cold cereal in the rain. It streamed off our faces and into our bowls. Dolly was parked right over us and going nowhere fast.

Staying put wasn't an option. We needed to get back on the river and find a place to wait out the storm.

"Too bad my dad is missing this," Rio said. "The river is really cooking. I hope you can handle the canoe. It's going to be a challenge."

"I can handle what we're looking at from here," I told him. "Around the next corner, I'll have to wait and see."

"Hey, don't feel like you have to try it. We can hide the canoe. When my dad gets back from Alaska, we can come back for it."

Rio was trying to keep it light, but he wasn't looking

me in the eye. He didn't think I could handle the canoe on this much water.

I took another look at the river. It was fast, real fast—pushier than I'd paddled back home, but not by much. And besides . . . I'd come out here to do some whitewater canoeing, and what I'd seen up to this point didn't even qualify.

"I'll let you know," I said with more bravado than I felt.

"Good for you. I'm sure it will be a blast." Rio didn't look convinced.

"We'll see how far I get. You'll be out in front to catch me if I capsize."

After girding for battle, we took a last-minute look at the upcoming miles in the guidebook. Good thing the pages were waterproof—the rain was constant. A mile around the corner, at Mile 30, we would leave the scaly mountain slopes behind. For the next forty miles, we would be in a tight corridor the river had incised in solid limestone, the fifteen-hundred-foot-deep Lower Canyons of the Rio Grande. That's where the rapids were waiting.

At Mile 34, where Oso Canyon entered from the Mexican side, the river ran under an overhanging bluff. "Use caution at higher water levels," the guidebook warned.

At Mile 36, a huge cave would appear on the Mexican side, the *"Cueva de la Puerta Grande."*

The first rapid we would come to was waiting at Mile 38. It was rated only Class 1 on the 1-to-6 scale.

The first of the major rapids was at Mile 40, at San

Rosendo Canyon. It was rated a 3 or a 4 depending on conditions. *Ouch.* Class 4 was for kayaks, not canoes.

"We'll take it as it comes," Rio said. "We'll go to shore for anything that needs to be scouted."

I remembered a mantra I had learned at canoe camp, a saying meant to dispel fear and the mental paralysis that comes with it: "Breathe. Organize. Act." I closed my eyes and took half a dozen slow, deep breaths. I remembered another saying that went, "Stay calm, be brave, and wait for the signs."

When I felt calmer, I opened my eyes. Rio was standing by the raft, waiting on me. I had the red canoe rigged just how I wanted it. The brand name emblazoned on the bow—Mad River—couldn't have been more apropos.

I was organized and I was ready. My rain top was zipped and my life jacket was cinched tight with rescue knife in place. My hat was snug. It was time to act. "I'm good to go," I announced. "Let me help you launch the raft."

We launched onto a river moving by like an express train. A few strokes from shore, and it was like I'd hooked onto a cable.

My heart was buoyant. With that paddle in my hands, it all came back to me—everything I loved about rivers. There's magic in moving water. Understanding what the water is doing, making those split-second moves you have to make to put yourself in the right place at the right time, you feel in tune with yourself and the whole Blue Planet. This was what I'd come for.

"Everything good?" Rio yelled.

"Better than that!" I yelled back. "Yee-haw!"

The river was running so fast, it took us no time at all to round the right-hand turn a mile downstream. We entered the gate of the Lower Canyons, with walls of limestone towering on both sides. My cousin had never been here before, same as me. Together, we were doing something epic, paddling into a tropical storm, no less.

Was I nuts?

Yes.

Did I have any regrets?

Ask me later.

As if we needed any more drama the wind began to blow, and blow hard. The clouds darkened, lowered, and swirled chaotically. A stupendous bolt of lightning accompanied by simultaneous and deafening thunder rent the canyon right down to the river, no more than a mile ahead. Five cows and a bull came stampeding upriver, spooked out of their skulls. The skies opened up and poured rain more intense than I'd seen in my life.

"*Hello, Dolly,*" I sang. "*Well, hello, Dolly.*" My mother loved that tune.

I could also hear my dad singing one of his Bob Dylan lines. He had one for every occasion. I sang along: "*Buckets of rain, buckets of tears, got all them buckets comin' out of my ears.*"

The torrents kept coming. I didn't need to reach for my water bottle. All I had to do was tilt my head back and open my mouth. The night rain had been merely a lull.

The sun was cooking Dolly's topside, and she was riled up but good. Rio thought she might be stalled and sucking up even more fuel from the Gulf of Mexico.

What a show. More lightning, more thunder, and waterfalls pouring over the canyon rims all the way down to the river. Some of them ran yellow, some brown, some red. The waterfalls were everywhere, falling a thousand feet and more.

We had a lot of dodging to do. With all the flash flooding, the river was running with debris, every sort of thorny shrub and scrubby tree. Even deeply rooted salt cedars had fallen in.

As fast as we were going, the canyon walls were flying by. It wasn't long before we saw Oso Canyon entering from the right. Rio motioned me alongside to make sure I was on top of the situation. The mile-by-mile guide had warned us to stay off the Mexican side, where the river at high water ran under a head-chopping ledge.

As we drew closer to the side canyon, we gave each other plenty of elbow room. Rio took a wide-left run, far from the head-chopper, and I did the same. The waves were wild, but I was able to reach out and brace on them when necessary, and apply power strokes when I needed to climb over their crests.

Dolly kept it up. She was throwing everything she had at us. It was getting harder and harder to see our way through the windblown sheets of rain. Some of the gusts were so strong, they picked up the water off the river and threw it in our faces. There was more and more debris in the river.

I pulled alongside Rio. "This is crazy!" I yelled.

The rain was spilling off his bedraggled straw hat like he was standing in the shower. "Totally," he yelled back.

We rounded a corner and spied the cave, a huge yawning void fairly low in the cliffs on the Mexican side—*La Cueva de la Puerta Grande*, The Cave of the Great Door. The door was more than great; it was immense.

We agreed in a nanosecond that we should check it out. We were in dire need of a safe, dry place.

At normal water levels, it might have been tough to find a break in the cane anywhere near the cave. But the cane was flooded, and we floated over its tassel tops. We landed in a boiling eddy at the foot of the slope falling from the mouth of the cave. Rio jumped from his raft, tie-rope in hand. He went down hard on the muddy bank, and for a second it looked like the river had him. He managed to scramble up and over the bank without letting go of the rope. "You okay?" I yelled.

"I'm okay!" he hollered as he ran limping to tie up.

With the raft safely secured to a boulder, Rio limped back to help me land. I tossed him my rope and he steadied the canoe as I stepped out. "Safely off the river!" he declared, all pumped up. "Give me five!"

"You hurt your knee?"

"Yeah, but it's nothing."

We clambered up the muddy slope, seventy feet or more, to the mouth of the cave. It was horizontal across the top and vertical down both sides, square as a door frame. What an amazing sensation it was to suddenly step onto dry ground, out of the weather and under the protection of that massive ceiling of limestone.

We still had some more climbing to do. We could only hope that the slope inside the cave would lead to some usable ground above.

What we found up there was way better than that. We came upon an almost perfect circle of hard-packed dirt maybe a hundred feet in diameter. Here and there lay a few rock slabs fallen from the ceiling, but otherwise the ground was smooth as the infield of a baseball diamond. At the rear wall we found ancient pictographs—a snake, a scorpion, a hand, and a crescent moon.

I'd never felt so removed from modern times or so connected to people from the distant past. It was like I was sheltering in this cave thousands of years before, looking down through sheets of rain to the swollen river during a flood just like this one.

"This is a whole other river than I've ever seen," Rio marveled. "This is the river that carved these canyons."

"At the moment, the *Rio Bravo* looks more berserk than brave."

"Right on. The word *bravo* is closer to berserk than brave. *Bravo* means 'fierce.'"

"You mean, your middle name means fierce, not brave?"

"You got it, *primo*. *Bravo* is a word you use to describe something wild and aggressive, like a bull running amok.

When the conquistadors named this river, it was probably flooding, something like now. *Rio Bravo*. Fierce River."

We decided to bring everything up from the boats that we would need for an extended stay. We had given ourselves nine nights, ten days given the likelihood of low water throughout the journey. As it was, we were well ahead of schedule. We could wait out the storm here and get back on a falling river with plenty of time to spare.

I went aboard the raft and began to hand the gear up to Rio. Once the raft was empty, we would be able to carry it to higher ground well out of reach of the river.

We were nearly done with the unloading when we heard a shout. We looked upstream through the rain and saw a rowboat. A dark-haired man was at the oars and a dark-haired boy sat on the front thwart.

The metal rowboat was pitching and bucking in the heavy water. The boy was tossing out water with a plastic milk jug converted into a bailer. "It's them," I said. "Carlos and Diego."

"In a rowboat, without life jackets!" Rio exclaimed. "That's insane!"

It Was All a Lie

CARLOS HAD US SPOTTED and was trying to row to shore from the middle of the river. The rowboat was going by almost in a blur. I didn't think he had a chance of breaking into the eddy. Strong as he was, though, he was gaining on it.

At the last second the coyote managed to row out of the mainstream current and into the water surging upriver. At the moment, he was at the foot of the eddy and we were at its head, fifty yards upstream. He rested a second or two, staring at us, before he realized he needed to row, and row hard, to have any chance of landing his boat. Before he could act, a huge sucking whirlpool grabbed hold of the rowboat and spun it twice around before spitting it out. By the time Carlos got his bearings and put his oars back in the water, he was halfway up the eddy.

The current in the eddy was nearly as powerful as the current out on the river. It shot him upstream and past us, no closer to shore than fifty feet. At the head of the eddy, the mainstream current grabbed hold of him once more, and down the river the rowboat went like it had been shot out of a bow.

Would he be able to pull into the eddy for a second try? I didn't want any part of his wrath, but for the boy's sake, I had to hope they made it. Without a life jacket, Diego was doomed to drown if they didn't.

The coyote rowed hard, Diego bailing all the while. For the second time, Carlos was able to pull into the eddy. The big whirlpool caught the rowboat once again, but not as squarely. He escaped it sooner.

This time, as he shot upstream, Carlos was angling toward the shore. Was he going to make it?

It was going to be close. I grabbed one of the gear straps and flew to the front of the raft with it, passing it under the grab line. I thought I might be able to attach the strap to the rowboat if I was quick enough. Their boat would be attached to ours, and ours was tied to a boulder.

Carlos didn't know much about rowing. He was pushing with his oars instead of pulling, and that was a mistake. You can't exert nearly the power when you're pushing. "Closer!" I yelled, beckoning him in. "Closer, closer!"

Carlos yelled something at Diego in Spanish. Diego grabbed their tie-rope and threw it at me, but it went nowhere, just landed in the water. Carlos, with a few last pushes, was closing the gap. I leaned out as far as I could, ready to run my strap through the ring in the prow of the rowboat.

Diego crouched in the front of the boat, holding on with a death grip. Then he wasn't holding on at all. He rose and leaned forward, reaching out toward me with both hands. I saw hope in his eyes, I saw desperation. He was close, but not close enough. They weren't going to make it.

Suddenly, in the pouring rain, Diego scrambled onto the tossing rowboat's triangular prow. He balanced there for a precarious instant, then leaped. I tried to catch him, but he fell into the river. I had a piece of him, though—I had him by the wrist. He reached with his other hand, and I hoisted him up to the raft.

The rowboat swept on by. Carlos looked stunned. Then he looked angry, extremely angry. At the head of the eddy, the surging river grabbed hold of the rowboat once again and sent it hurtling downstream. Carlos quit rowing; he must've been spent. The river shot him around the corner and out of sight.

I helped the boy out of the raft. Diego's chest was heaving, and he was sobbing uncontrollably. It was all he could do to stand. "You're okay; everything will be okay," I told him.

His eyes, looking downstream, were full of fear. "Everything he told you was a lie," Diego sobbed. "I could not warn you. He said he would kill me, kill both of you, if I even looked at you."

"Don't worry," Rio said. "I don't think you'll see him again. We'll take care of you, Diego."

"It was all a lie! My mother is not in Chicago . . . he is no coyote. My mother is in Mexico City. My name is Diego Cervantes. I was with my father at a hotel in the mountains . . ."

Diego covered his eyes with his forearm and nearly crumpled to the ground. I had never seen anybody so overcome. "You don't have to—," I started to say.

The boy brushed his tears away. He needed to talk. "I was outside when it happened. My father was inside with the other two judges. I heard shooting, so much shooting inside the building. Four men with war rifles but no uniforms ran out of the lodge. One was this Carlos—"

Diego heaved for breath and went on. "A security man came to help—all he had was a small pistol. He wounded one of the criminals. Carlos killed him with many bullets right before my eyes. Carlos and the other three, they ran all different ways. More guards came, more shooting. I tried to run away but Carlos, he grabbed me and ran into the forest. He knew who I was! By then I figured out who they were: criminals who work for the drug lords and kill for money. I tried to break loose, but he knocked me down. That's when he dropped the rifle and used his pistol instead. Watch out—he still has it! It shoots many bullets very fast. Two guards followed but they were afraid to shoot because of me. Carlos put a cloth through my mouth and dragged me with him. Too many trees, too many rocks, too many places to hide. Helicopters came much later. I saw them, but they never saw me."

"It's okay," I told Diego. "It's going to be okay."

"It's not going to be okay!" he wailed. "They killed my father. I know it!"

I knelt next to him and pulled him close. He bawled his eyes out. "You don't know for sure," I said. "You said you weren't inside. Your father could have survived."

Rio and I weren't comforted by my hollow words, and neither was Diego. He told us his mother had always been afraid this would happen. Sooner or later it happened to everyone who stood up to the drug cartels.

"My father is honest," Diego sobbed. "So were the other two judges who came to the mountains with us. They don't take the bribes. They put the drug lords into prison for the rest of their lives. In Mexico City, we live in fear. So many kidnappings. My sisters and I go to the international school in an armored car. At the school, there are guards at every door."

"You're safe now," I told him.

"How can you say that? Carlos has that pistol in his backpack, with extra ammunition. What if he comes back?"

"He got swept away," Rio said. "I really don't think he could get back here even if he tried. We're going to camp in the cave. Make something to eat. You've been brave, really brave. Let's get you out of the rain and the wind."

We grabbed some gear and took Diego up to the cave. We left him with an energy bar and water, and went back to the boats. We carried the raft and the canoe well out of reach of the floodwater. All the while, we kept looking over our shoulders. "You really think he couldn't make it to shore?" I asked.

"It's a minor miracle he made it this far in that rowboat. There's a rapid around the bend. Most likely he got swept into it and capsized. Without a life jacket, he's history."

"He stole the rowboat from the wax makers way upstream, don't you figure, Rio?"

"For sure. He must've had it hidden nearby when he walked into camp yesterday morning. The Black Hawk patrolling the river never spotted him because he was floating at night. It wouldn't have been that hard to do. The moon was up, and there weren't any rapids. During the day he probably had the boat hidden in the cane."

"I'm afraid there's not much hope for Diego's father. At the house where the baby was born, didn't you hear that the judges were killed?"

"I did, but all the same, it's good you told Diego not to give up hope."

When we got back to the cave with our second load, Diego shared another fear with us. The cartels always killed the people they kidnapped, even children, if their families couldn't pay the ransom. His family wasn't wealthy.

Rio and I left the cave to fetch the rest of our camp gear. We weighted the raft and canoe with smooth stones to make sure that a gust of wind wouldn't pick them up and throw them on the sharp limestone boulders, the cactus, or the catclaw mesquite. Our rescue knives from our life jackets were all we had in the way of weapons. We unclipped them, scabbards and all, and put them in the deep front pockets of our lightweight desert trousers. They were better than nothing.

Back in the cave, we set up the table and chairs. A flat, knee-high rock served as a third chair. We rigged the stove and gas bottle, spread our tarp on the ground, and set out our cooking stuff. We also brought out all our remaining food items. It wasn't a very impressive inventory, but we weren't going to starve.

There'd be no skimping this evening, that was for sure. We were going to use three of our soup packets—Diego chose chicken noodle—and make a big pot of pasta. Diego gave the nod to the four-cheese sauce packet to flavor it. We ate our fill looking out the mouth of the cave, through the unceasing rain, to the flooding river. A big cottonwood tree floated by. No doubt Rio and Diego were thinking the same thing I was: The slope below the cave was so steep, we wouldn't be able to see Carlos if he was sneaking up on us. It would also be impossible to hear him, with the cave roof amplifying the sound of the river.

After we rinsed our plates and put away the dishes, Rio brought out his cards. We taught Diego how to play Hearts, and he caught on fast after a couple of rounds. After four rounds, with Rio in the lead, the light at the back of the grotto was getting dimmer and dimmer. Diego grew increasingly anxious, glancing at the mouth of the cave as if his tormenter would appear at any moment.

Rio fished a new trick from the bottom of his dry bag—a couple of candles. The candlelight had a soothing effect on Diego, and we kept playing. It wasn't until it was pitch-dark outside the cave, with Diego in second place, that we called it a day. We put away the things we had spread out on the tarp, inflated our ground pads, and lay down to sleep. Rio was the odd man out. He claimed that a kid from Terlingua didn't need a ground pad.

Sandwiched between the two of us, Diego fell asleep fast. He had an angel's face. It broke my heart to think he would wake to the loss of his father.

Good Morning, Texas

COME MORNING THE RIVER was running higher yet, but the rain had stopped, and so had the wind. The skies were still leaden. Had Dolly moved on by, or was this merely the intermission before Act Two?

We ate breakfast, the last of the cold cereal. Out of earshot of the boy, Rio and I talked strategy. Here's the question we kept coming back to: Did it make sense to sit tight and see if Dolly was gone for good, with even a small chance that Carlos was stalking us as we spoke?

We decided to get back on the river and put a bunch of miles behind us—twenty, thirty, even forty. Given the speed of the river, it might even be possible to make it all the way—forty-seven miles—to the takeout at Dryden Crossing. We would arrive days early, but the upside would be huge. The three of us would be safely off the river, and a pinpointed manhunt for Carlos could begin.

By ten in the morning, with the clouds darkening ominously and thunder beginning to rumble, we had the raft and canoe rigged. Our spare life jacket was too large for Diego, but we managed to secure it snugly by attaching it to a harness around his waist and crotch that we improvised with extra raft straps.

We put our own life jackets on, clipped our rescue knives in place, and got out the guidebook. Hot Springs Rapid, a 3 or a 4 at normal levels, was waiting four miles downstream. "It might be all washed out," Rio said. "Then again, it might've turned into a monster."

From behind us, just then, from the rock where we'd left Diego sitting, came a sudden cry like the squeal of a small animal about to be slaughtered.

We spun around, and there was Carlos, with one hand around the boy's neck. The other held a big pistol, and the pistol was pointed at us. "Good morning, Texas," he cackled. "Good morning, Carolina! Hello, my friends, did you sleep well?"

His arms and his face looked even worse than before, like he'd battled the river and lost, but the evil grin on his face said otherwise, and he still had his backpack. "What's the matter, boys? Cat got your tongues?"

Diego squirmed, broke free, and ran to us. I held him to me. He buried his face in my life jacket. He was too frightened to even look.

Carlos taunted him in Spanish. I think he called him a scared rabbit, a frightened little chicken.

"Take those knives off your life jackets, boys, holders

and all, and toss them over here. You toss them anywhere else and I will shoot one of you dead as an example to the other. It will be you, Carolina. I'll keep Texas alive to row the raft down to San Rosendo Canyon, where I asked you boys to take me in the first place. You should have done as I asked, no? What's keeping you? Toss the knives over here now!"

We did as he said. He stepped forward and picked them up, his pistol on us all the while. He clipped the knives to his belt, one on each hip.

The killer sneered at us. "Now the book."

Diego whimpered. I felt like whimpering, too. All I could think of was how idiotic I had been all along, starting with hitchhiking from Alpine to Terlingua. Not calling my parents from the Starlight, not telling them my uncle was in Alaska, not giving them the chance to tell me to come straight home if they thought it was best. Why didn't I even give them the chance?

Carlos sat down on a rock with the guidebook, pistol at his side, and began to flip through the pages. He grinned when he found the page he was looking for. "Only four miles from the cave to my road up San Rosendo Canyon. The book says that the road is an 'illegal immigration highway.' I like the sound of that. Sounds like a good place for me and my little chicken to catch a ride."

"We could let you off there," Rio said, "but the road is not the kind of highway you're thinking about—just a rough four-wheel-drive track. Chances are, it's been destroyed in the last twenty-four hours. All the side canyons have been flash-flooding, and San Rosendo Canyon is the biggest one on the Mexican side. You can look it up. San Rosendo is flooding for sure."

I could see what Rio was doing: building the case for Carlos keeping us alive. He would need us to take him farther down the river.

"We'll find out soon," Carlos said with a smirk. "It's good to be traveling with an expert such as yourself. This Hot Springs Rapid, where San Rosendo Canyon meets the river . . . the book says it's Class 3 or Class 4. How high do the numbers go, Texas?"

"Five means expert kayakers and rafters can attempt it, but it's extremely dicey. Six means don't even think about it. But the numbers in this book mean nothing during a flood. They only apply up to five or six thousand cubic feet per second, which is as high as the man who wrote the book ever saw. What we've got in the river now is probably five times that much water, maybe more."

"I got this far in a rowboat," Carlos scoffed. "All the same, I want you to row the raft the next four miles."

"How come, if you had no problem with the rowboat? Take a look. The only rapid between here and there is only Class 1. Did you have a problem in that rapid with the rowboat yesterday?"

"Enough of this," the thug barked. "Throw me your life jacket, Carolina."

Rio unbuckled his, and tossed it. "Here, take mine. Dylan is in the canoe, and the canoe is more likely to capsize."

Carlos laughed. "Okay by me, Texas. After all, I'll be with you. If you have no life jacket, you'll be extra careful with the raft. It's not only my little chicken's life you need to watch out for. Why the long faces, boys? Did you find out that little Diego can speak after all? Speak English, even? Did my little chicken keep you up last night telling wild stories about me? Did he tell you what happens to judges who are too stupid to take the big money that would enable their families to live well for the rest of their lives?"

Rio feigned surprise. "What are you talking about? He told us he wished you would take him to his mother in Chicago after all, instead of back to his grandmother in Mexico."

"Watch your step, Texas," Carlos snarled. "You're in the bullring with no sword. Untie the raft, both of you together. Then turn it around so I can step into the front with the little chicken under my wing. When we get to San Rosendo Canyon, don't do anything stupid or I will dump your bullet-ridden carcasses in the *Rio Bravo*. Do you understand me, Carolina?"

"I understand," I answered, trying to disguise my terror.

"Do you understand me, Texas?"

"*Sí*," Rio muttered.

"Carolina! Did you hear that? Your *primo* just copped an attitude. Texas shouldn't have done that. It makes me suspicious of him, deeply suspicious. As for you, Carolina, I have some old gangster wisdom for you. We have a saying that goes like this: *Desconfía de tu mejor amigo como de tu peor enemigo*. Trust your best friend as you would your worst enemy."

The monster waved his big pistol and laughed derisively. He picked the life jacket up and put it on, slowly and one-handed. Lightning snapped downriver, its thunderclap reverberating through the canyon as we went to untie the boats.

At the trunk of the mesquite where we had tied, Rio and I knelt to get at the knots. "Should we land above Hot Springs, or blow through the rapid?" Rio whispered.

"Tell me what you're thinking," I whispered back.

"If I'm wrong about the road being washed out, he has no reason to keep us alive."

"If you don't try to pull out before the rapid, or pretend you can't, how's he going to react to that?"

"Not sure . . . he's capable of anything."

"Hurry up, you clowns!" Carlos yelled.

"Time's running out, Dylan."

"You play it by ear, Rio, and we'll hope for the best."

"If he decides to try to hike out, I think he'll hedge his bets and take us with him. It's twelve miles to that ranch. If he doesn't make it and has to turn back to the river, he'll still need us. I'll make sure he knows there will be more rapids as bad as Hot Springs so he doesn't start thinking he can row the raft."

By now we both had our knots undone. I couldn't speak; I could barely breathe. I returned to the canoe in a fog of fear. The rain broke loose.

"*Vamanos, muchachos!*" our tormenter cackled. "Hop to, let's get in the boats. Down the *Rio Bravo* I go, with two rabbits and a chicken!"

You Can't Get There from Here

DOLLY WAS FAR FROM done. We flew down the canyon into the teeth of the redoubled storm. Lightning struck upstream and down. Torrents of rain slashed at us, and the wind-tossed waves attacked from all sides. Waterfalls even more spectacular than before cascaded from the canyon rims.

As we rounded the corner a mile below the cave, I slid off my seat and into the whitewater position, my knees spread wide against the hull of the canoe. I had a Class 1 rapid to put behind me. It was coming up soon, where Silber Canyon entered from the Texas side.

On a day like this, with a major rapid lying in wait only a few miles on, a Class 1 tune-up was okay by me.

Suddenly the side canyon came into view. A second later I heard the roar of flash flooding. A couple of heartbeats after that and I saw how much water Silber Canyon was dumping into the Rio Grande—hugely more than the Rio Grande itself had been running when we set out on this ill-fated adventure.

I drew a deep breath. Rio was already starting down the tongue of the rapid. The wave train waiting for him below was enormous, like a succession of rearing, white-maned horses. Class 1? No way. Class 3 was more like it.

I've got a spray cover, I told myself. I'm not gonna swamp. I'm also not gonna capsize. You ran Class 3 rapids back home, and you got pretty good at it.

I took a quick glimpse below to see how Rio was faring. He was riding the wave train like a roller coaster, keeping the raft straight while pushing through the troughs and over the top of each exploding wave. My eyes went to Diego, up front in the raft with Carlos, hanging on as best he could. Carlos wasn't helping him. Carlos had one hand on the grab line that ran around the raft; the other was pointing a gun at his boatman. How insane was that for Rio?

Almost too late, I focused on my own situation. I was starting down the tongue. It was steep and it was fast. There wasn't a chance in the world Carlos had made it through this rapid with the rowboat. He must have rowed to shore above it or swam to shore below it.

Down the narrowing tongue I went. I had to hit every roller in the wave train just right: up and down and up and down and up and down until I was all the way through. A moment's lapse and I would capsize.

I rose onto the first wave. I had never climbed a wave this high. I paddled hard to get over the top and nearly spilled in a cascade of whitewater. Leaning to my right and reaching with my paddle blade, I was able to brace on the wave, or I would have gone over.

My roller coaster was only beginning. With the rain in my face, I battled for position in every trough, fought to stay upright over the summit of every crashing wave.

I got a cheer from my cousin, parked in the eddy, as I flew past them. Diego was safely inside the raft. So was the man with the gun.

I was able to pull into the bottom of the eddy and ride it upstream to the raft. I brought the canoe alongside.

Rio pumped his fist. "Big-time, Dylan, big-time!"

"So far, so good," I allowed. I reached for my bailer and started tossing out water. My spray covers had saved me from swamping, but even so, some of the waves had splashed into the canoe on account of the uncovered section immediately around me. The gunman's face, watching me bail while keeping track of Rio, was all calculation, cold calculation.

Diego was trembling, and not from the cold.

My cousin got back to business. "San Rosendo Canyon is going to come up fast, Dylan. The river should pool up at the top of Hot Springs Rapid. We'll take out and scout on the right side, like the book says. Don't jam me, or I won't have time to land and catch you when you come in. And don't float into the rapid, no matter what. You won't have any protection waiting downstream if you do."

"Got it," I said.

"But if the river doesn't pool up above the rapid, and we can't get to the shore, I'll have to run it and so will you."

Diego's face quickened with terror. The face of his kidnapper betrayed uncertainty, suspicion, and hatred. He hated us, and he hated the lack of total control.

Rio's jaw was clenched as he pulled back into the current. He didn't seem at a loss, like me, and he didn't appear to be sick to his stomach. How could he not be thinking of his father, like I suddenly found myself thinking of my parents, my sisters, and my brother? Did he actually believe we were going to live through this?

Clench your own jaw, and don't make any stupid mistakes. You might have to run Hot Springs at flood stage, real soon.

The rain slackened somewhat. The next few miles flew by all too fast. We might've been going ten miles an hour. After a long, straight run, the river jogged right, then left. A deep cleft in the Lower Canyons appeared on the Mexican side—San Rosendo Canyon already.

At the mouth of the deep side canyon, the Rio Grande appeared to be coming to a dead end. That wasn't possible. It meant the river was bending sharply left at the top of Hot Springs Rapid.

Rio swept ever closer to the brink, me following closer than I would have liked. Where was the eddy water, so I could put on the brakes?

Suddenly we had a strong wind at our backs, and

driving rain again, right when we could've used a break. "You're inhuman, Dolly," I muttered, and laughed at my weak attempt at gallows humor.

Focus, I commanded myself, hearing the full-throated roar of Hot Springs Rapid. Whitewater was spitting up from below the first drop. The river was pooling up behind the brink of the rapid as Rio had predicted. We should be able to go to shore above the rapid and scout it.

As we drew ever closer, the roar of the rapid ever more ferocious, I had to fight hard to keep my stomach down. This was just too much.

There was no beach to land on, nothing like that. Everything was flooded. Rio found a landing spot, though, against a gigantic slab of limestone. Carlos stepped onto it, tie-rope in one hand and pistol in the other.

Carlos snubbed the raft against the boulder and told Diego to climb out. Diego did as he was told, and stood glassy-eyed in the rain. Carlos tied the raft to a nearby mesquite. Rio helped me land the canoe alongside the raft. "I sure hope San Rosendo is flash-flooding," he whispered. "Too bad we can't tell from here."

Carlos returned to the raft. His backpack was on the front thwart, and he wanted Rio to hand it out to him, slowly. Rio did as he was told. The backpack was heavy, I noticed, with what was left of the canned meat we had given him, his extra ammunition clips, and maybe a jug of water.

"Take care of Diego," Rio said to Carlos, as if in parting.

"Nice try, Texas," Carlos replied with heavy sarcasm.

"You two are going with us all the way to that ranch house. If I can't get any help there, we're coming back to your boat for a ride down the river. You're stuck with me until I say different."

"Okay by me," Rio said almost cheerfully. "We can help make sure Diego gets out safely."

"Let's go see what shape the road is in. We all go together, you two clowns in front."

I strapped the canoe to the side of the raft and stepped to the shore. Carlos gave us a wide berth and told us to take the lead. I followed Rio through the brush. It was a short walk but hard to get through unscathed in the rain. Rio slipped in the mud and went down on the knee he'd injured previously. A catclaw mesquite raked the back of my hand and drew blood.

The brush gave way as we approached the high, stony ground separating our landing spot from the side canyon. As we topped out, we were greeted by a monstrous roar. The mouth of San Rosendo Canyon, wall to wall, was filled with raging floodwater.

The kidnapper and his muddy captive joined us at our vantage point. Carlos cut loose with a torrent of Spanish curses.

"There's nothing left of the road," Rio said matter-of-factly.

"I see with my eyes, Texas. I don't need a fool to say the obvious. It will be harder without the road. We'll have to keep to high ground. Stay above the flood."

On our side of San Rosendo Canyon, that didn't seem

possible. The talus slopes below the cliffs were radically steep and choked with cactus and spear-sharp yuccas.

The killer's eyes were on the other side of San Rosendo Canyon. The slopes there were more barren and not nearly as steep. As far as we could see, that side of the canyon was walkable. The ranch Carlos was trying to get to, however, was twelve miles from the river. Who knows what we would run into.

"We'll try the other side," Carlos said.

Rio shook his head. "You can't get there from here."

"Not by foot, Texas."

"How, then?"

Carlos pointed to the Rio Grande, to Hot Springs Rapid, where the flood leaving the side canyon boiled into the far greater flood coming down the river. "The answer is obvious. You take us through the rapid, we land downstream, we hike up the other side of San Rosendo Canyon."

"Easier said than done, Carlos," Rio said coolly.

"I have confidence in you, Texas."

For the first time, I took a good look at Hot Springs Rapid. It was peppered with boat-eating holes where the whitewater poured over submerged boulders and back on itself.

Rio asked how it looked to me.

"Sick," I replied.

Ready, Boys?

HOT SPRINGS RAPID AT flood stage was scary enough. From our scouting spot it was a gut-wrenching sight. In the rain, with thunder rumbling and a gun at our backs, it was nothing short of terrifying. The rapid's first drop was a beast, and more hazards waited below. If I capsized, there'd be no swimming out of the current for as far as I could see, maybe a mile. "Too much jeopardy," I said over the roar of the rapid. "This has got to be Class 4."

Rio looked grim. "No doubt about it."

"I've met my match. What do you say we ditch the canoe, like you were saying we might have to? Are you sure you'll be able to come back for it with your dad, like you were talking about?"

"Pretty sure, but that doesn't matter. Getting home

alive is the only thing."

"Ready, boys?" Carlos called mockingly.

I glanced at Rio. "You pretty sure you can take the raft through this?"

"If I enter the sweet spot we should be okay."

My cousin and I started down the trail to the boats. Carlos followed, holding Diego back.

I untied the canoe. Rio pulled it halfway out of the water. "What are you two doing?" yelled Carlos.

Rio explained that the rapid was too dangerous to attempt in a canoe. We were going to leave it behind.

Carlos thought about that for about two seconds. "Oh no, you don't," he said with a toothy smile.

"It's a good deal all around," I hastened to say. "I can hang on to Diego—make sure he stays in the raft."

Diego brightened at the idea. Carlos scowled. "Good try, Carolina. That last rapid . . . you looked like a pro! You're afraid, that's all. Suck it up, kid! I want to see how you do when you're paddling for your life!"

"Carlos," Rio intervened. "All of us need to work together if we're going to get through this."

"Save it, Texas! You have no idea who you are talking to!"

"If I could just explain," I put in, trying to appear calm. "This is Class 4 water. I would if I could, but I can't."

"You'll try anyway. This will be fun."

"Fun?"

"Fun for me to watch. You have a life jacket. What's the big deal?"

"Life jacket or no, it's too dangerous. Tell you what, I'll ride in the back of the raft."

"You don't tell *me* anything," Carlos hissed. "I tell *you*. You don't get it, Carolina. What do I need with you? One idiot is easier to keep track of than two. If you keep this up, I'm going to shut your mouth forever."

The hit man pointed the big pistol at my heart.

"He'll do it!" Diego cried. "Dylan, he'll kill you!"

"With pleasure," Carlos added.

"On second thought," I said with a grim laugh, "I think I can paddle this rapid."

Rio eased the canoe back into the water. He put his hand on my shoulder and looked me in the eye. "I know you can, *primo*. Just follow my route."

The killer waved me into the canoe with his pistol. Rio saw to Diego's life jacket and the harness we had attached it to, pulling the straps tight. "Stay brave," he told the boy.

Diego fought to keep from crying. "I'll try," he promised.

Rio went to the mesquite and untied the raft. The rain beat down ever harder. He returned to the raft so deep in thought, he appeared to be in a trance. He looked fierce, and much older than fifteen. I realized how much I had been counting on him all the way down the river. What was he thinking, now that we were totally up against it?

Carlos had already taken the boy to the front of the raft, but was hesitant to sit down. Rio knelt on the shore, securing the coiled tie-rope at the stern. "Put your gun away," he called to Carlos. "Neither you nor Diego has a chance of staying in the raft unless you do. Stay in the center of the boat, on the cross tube, and hold on the best you can."

"With my back to you, Texas? That's not gonna happen."

"If you're gonna sit on the side of the raft, sit in front of Diego, so your body will shield him from the waves. No bailing is required; this is a self-bailing raft. Your only job is to hang on to him!"

Carlos sat where he pleased, on the outside tube, then yanked Diego into place.

Rio launched the raft. It was already drifting up the eddy as he stepped forward into the boatman's compartment.

I pivoted the canoe and followed him up the eddy. "You can do it, Dylan!" he called. "I've got you covered. Keep an eye out for Diego in case he's in the river!"

"Got it," I croaked. I felt weak all over. I couldn't even swallow, my throat was so dry. I suddenly noticed a blister from that last rapid. It was on my right forefinger, and had already torn open without me even knowing it was there. Suddenly it was killing me.

I took a deep breath, and another. I slid off the seat onto my knees. I braced them against the hull. "Keep low," I reminded myself. "Keep your balance."

Rio was at the top of the eddy. He waited until I wasn't so far behind him, gave me a thumbs-up, and pulled onto the current.

As I left the eddy water, the current took me so violently I nearly tipped over. Barely in time, I righted the canoe and paddled to catch up. This was going to go fast.

You can do this, I told myself, but only if you believe you can. Your spray covers, front and back, will keep most of the water out. Get in tune with the river. Stay calm, be brave, you're going to live through this. Paddle strong, do your thing the best you're able.

All the while, I was visualizing the rapid, which I wouldn't be able to see until the last second. Enter right of center, try to walk the line between the wave train and the huge hole on the right side. After that, "read and run."

Rio was closing fast on the brink. I saw Carlos stuff the pistol under his waistband. He passed one arm behind Diego's back and took hold of the grab line with both hands. Diego's hands were at his sides, with a tight grip on the grab line. He looked over his shoulder at me, his face a frozen mask.

I tugged on the cinches at the side of my life jacket. They were good and tight.

The river was bending hard to the left. I wondered if Rio was going to be able to enter right of center, where he intended. The overwhelmingly powerful current was pulling him left. Unless he could break out of it, he was going to be out of position. The raft would flip for certain as soon as he went over the edge.

Rio cocked the raft to the left and pulled hard to the right, hard as he could. I was afraid he had waited too long, and wouldn't have time to pivot the boat and take the drop straight on.

He was gaining on it, and finally he was right where he needed to be. At the last second he executed the pivot and straightened out. The raft disappeared over the brink with the bow pointed directly downstream.

I adjusted while I still could. The brink of the rapid was a horizon line clear across the river. I couldn't see over it, not yet. It felt like I was about to go over the edge of the world.

Suddenly I could see it all. I saw the disaster hole on the far left, with its monster backlash off the limestone slab. I saw the enormous wave train down the center. Rio was on it, and he was upright, four or five waves down. I saw a vicious hole underneath the brink on my right and the powerful whirlpool beyond it.

Most of all, I could see the tightrope I needed to walk between the wave train and the hazards on the right side. My path for the next fifty yards was no more than three feet wide. I was going to have to stay right on it.

Over the edge I went—down, down, down. I fought to stay off the wave train that Rio had ridden. Never had I seen the likes of those churning haystacks of violent whitewater. I had to keep right of that whole roller coaster.

With quick strokes and strong braces, leaning into my danger when the waves attacked from the side, this balancing act was taking everything I had.

So far, so good. I was fighting my way through an obstacle course. It was all I could do to avoid the reversals where the river was pouring over submerged boulders. Drop into one of them and I was done.

I caught a glimpse of Rio. He was done with the wave train and halfway through the tail waves. And now he was cocking the boat to start pulling for the Mexican shore.

Rio was still working right, and closing in on the shore. Me, no way. I was lucky not to be swimming. My canoe was out in the middle of the river and passing him by.

As soon as my cousin saw I wasn't going to be able to land, he leaned on the oars, pivoted the raft, and started pulling back toward the center of the river. I saw Carlos leap up with the gun and yell at Rio. Rio yelled back at him. Carlos pointed the gun, threatening to shoot. Rio ignored him and kept rowing. He was going to cover me no matter what.

I couldn't get any closer to shore. I had taken a scary amount of water into my open cockpit, and lost most of my maneuverability. With waves still crashing, a time-out for bailing was out of the question. If I quit paddling, I would swamp completely. As it was, I kept taking water, and the canoe was wallowing badly. Where was an eddy when I needed one?

As the river bent to the right, a cliff wall loomed on the Mexican side. Hundreds of feet high, it soared straight out of the river. If I couldn't get to shore before that wall, the cliff would make it impossible to hike back to San Rosendo Canyon. Carlos would be furious if he couldn't hike out to that ranch.

Try as I might, it couldn't be done. The river swept me past the cliff.

The sheer wall, about a hundred yards long, stirred the river into a frenzy downstream—a huge, boiling eddy.

I struggled with everything I had to reach the eddy water. At the last second I was able to catch it. I rode it upstream to a small beach where the cliffs ended. I got out and dragged the canoe onto the shore. Rio was about to shoot on by. I hollered and waved my hat and hollered some more.

Rio spotted me and pulled with everything he had, trying to catch the eddy.

He caught it. It would take them a minute to float upstream to the beach where I waited, full of dread. What was Carlos going to do now?

I sucked on my forefinger, which was bleeding, and noticed that the rain had stopped. I looked skyward and noticed something. The clouds were racing, chased by another air mass. Downstream, between two cloudbanks, a seam of blue sky was showing.

My eyes went back to the raft. Diego had come through the rapid safely. That was something to be thankful for.

Carlos was boiling with rage.

What Did You Do That For?

EAPING FROM THE RAFT, pistol in hand, Carlos marched
straight at me. My eyes fell on that brutal scar that ran
from his forehead through his hairline. He ordered me
to my knees and pointed the gun at my head. His finger
was on the trigger. "You went by that cliff on purpose!"
he roared.

It was impossible to keep my voice from quavering.
"I did my best to get to shore. Honestly, I tried my best."

Rio sprang ashore, tie-rope in hand. The raft, with
Diego still aboard, was rocking in the eddy. Carlos glared
at Rio, glared at me. He glanced above the cliff to see if
there was a way to climb above it and get back to San
Rosendo Canyon.

When he saw there wasn't, he gave me a swift kick. I
saw it coming—right at my ribs. I fell back, taking only a

glancing blow. Carlos whirled and pointed the gun at Rio. "You deserve it more than him!"

"Where we landed, you came out ahead," Rio told him.

"How is that, Texas?"

"It just wasn't possible, trying to hike out by staying high. The road to that ranch followed the bottom of San Rosendo Canyon for a reason. A big canyon like San Rosendo has its own side canyons, and they would've stopped us for sure. We would've had to turn back. Maybe after two hours, maybe after two days. It would have been impossible."

The man holding the gun was cooling down, at least a little. "You're only guessing."

"It's an educated guess. I've lived in the Big Bend my whole life. The river is the easy way to travel, and look how fast it is right now. From here, we could be out of the canyons in a matter of hours. Look how much daylight is left. There'll be other roads into Mexico once we're past the canyons. The country won't be so rugged."

Still suspicious, Carlos was at least listening to reason. I could see it in his cruel features. This might be working out to his advantage after all.

Carlos ordered Diego to come ashore with the guidebook. Our captor retreated with it to a rock ledge at the back of the beach. He put the pistol down and began to turn the pages. For the time being, the storm in his brain seemed to have subsided. Rio, Diego, and I waited on the raft. We ate the last three energy bars.

The swallows began to work the river again, and the weather continued to improve. A magnificent double rainbow spanned the canyon downstream. Carlos looked to the sky with apprehension. I wondered why rapidly improving weather had him worried. The answer hit me: The storm had given him cover. Airplanes and helicopters would soon be able to fly again. He might not have much time left to get off the river and vanish into Mexico.

I ran this line of thought past Rio. He agreed, and said that Carlos was getting more and more desperate. We better figure out how to shake him, and soon. If a helicopter showed up—Big Bend's River Ranger might come looking for us—there was no telling what Carlos would do.

"What are you two jawing about?" Carlos barked.

"The rainbows . . . the weather," Rio said.

"Lots of rapids the next fifteen miles. Twelve miles from here is a rapid where it says, 'Bad at any level.'"

"Upper Madison Falls. Worst rapid on the Rio Grande. We'll have to go to shore and scout that one for sure."

"That's at Mile 55. It says the deep canyons end at Mile 63."

"That's right. Twenty miles downstream from here."

Slowly, Carlos kept turning the pages. Each map covered about five miles. "Yes, it's true, and the land is flatter, as you said. I see a few roads on the Mexican side, but there is no telling where they go."

"Ranches, would be my guess."

"But how far from the river are the ranches?"

"Don't know."

"Who is meeting you, and when?"

"A driver from Terlingua—I don't know who it's going to be—three days from now. We're ahead of schedule."

"What mile you get picked up?"

"Mile 83—Dryden Crossing. Forty miles from here."

Carlos turned another page and discovered something that made him smile. "Why didn't you tell me this before, Texas?"

"What's that, Carlos?"

"Half a mile before we get to your road at Dryden Crossing, there is a trail to a village in Mexico. The village of Agua Verde is only a mile from the river! There is a landing strip there, and a road south. Can you recognize the trail from the river?"

"If I was watching for it. I've never been through the Lower Canyons before. Just spent a lot of time looking at that guidebook, wishing I could."

"Wishing you could go through a rapid that's 'bad at any level'?"

"Most people portage."

"What does that mean?"

"Carry everything around the side. It takes hours. We would camp at the end of the portage. That's what my dad usually does."

"I don't think so . . . I couldn't get to Agua Verde today if we did that. Look, the storm is breaking up. I'm not staying on the river another day. I think you can row Upper Madison Falls, hot shot."

"I won't know till we get there."

"I agree," Carlos said with a sly grin. "Let's not waste time talking about it."

"Fine by me," Rio said. "Hold on a few minutes, though. The canoe is going to be nothing but trouble, as you've already seen. The water is just too big. See that brush downstream? Dylan and I will hide it in back of the brush . . . twenty minutes, no more, we'll be back."

"I'll think about it," Carlos said with the same sly grin. "There, I thought about it. You're right, Texas, that canoe is nothing but trouble, and your cousin shouldn't be risking his life in it."

He wheeled around with his pistol and sprayed a clip full of rounds down the length of the canoe, low along the hull. The sudden, shocking bursts from the fully automatic pistol registered with brutal effect.

Quickly, professionally, Carlos jammed a new clip into place.

"What did you do that for?" Rio demanded.

To remind us he's a murderer, I thought. Diego, who clung to my side, didn't need reminding.

Carlos laughed. "To save me twenty minutes. And to save you an extra trip to this wasteland to come and get it."

Carlos announced that I would take his place in the front of the raft and make sure his chicken stayed in the boat. Carlos would be riding on the tarped gear behind Rio, "because the view will be better from the back."

We were soon underway. I suppose I was in a state of shock. With so many bad rapids coming up, I should have felt fortunate to be riding in the raft. As it was, I felt numb. My whole life I had taken freedom for granted. There was nothing sweeter, unless it was life itself.

Diego and I sat on the front thwart, centered in the raft in front of Rio. I thought about something Diego had said, that kidnapping victims, children included, were always killed if their families couldn't make ransom. Somehow, when it came time to make our move—whatever that might be—we had to make sure we didn't leave Diego behind.

Was there any chance, at the end of the line, that this vermin would let the three of us go?

Why would he, knowing we would put the authorities on him first chance we got?

Bad at Any Level

IT ALL CAME DOWN to this: twenty more miles of the deep canyons, and twenty miles beyond. They were going to go fast, real fast. Rio told Carlos to hand him the mile-by-mile guide so he could read up on the rapids to come. Carlos did, grudgingly. When Rio immediately handed it forward to me, saying he had to keep his hands on the oars, Carlos cursed him, but let it go. His own hide was at stake.

As much to calm my own nerves as well as Rio's and Diego's, I filled them in on what we were seeing. The *Cañon Caballo Blanco*—the Canyon of the White Horse— came up quickly on the right. We were approaching the signature geological feature of the Lower Canyons: the Bullis Fold, where the layers of limestone, rising from the Texas side of the river to a height of sixteen hundred feet, are folded an eye-popping 90 degrees. Immediately before the fold, three canyons in quick succession would enter from the Texas side of the river. Directly under the fold, as the river takes a horseshoe bend, we would encounter Bullis Fold Rapid.

"Read me what it says about the rapid," Rio said tersely.

"Here goes: 'Bullis Fold Rapid, Class 2-plus. Beware of standing waves and unpredictable currents in these narrows. Dangerous whirlpools and logjams occur during floods. Exercise extreme caution.'"

"Thanks. That's what I needed to know."

As we rounded the corner, I spied the three canyons entering on our left, and dead ahead, at a sharp bend in the river, the Bullis Fold on the Texas side. It was quite a sight: layer upon layer of cliffy limestone shooting from the river, soaring, then folding into horizontal cliff bands with steep talus slopes in between.

Suddenly the entire spectacle was lit with glowing sunshine, the first to light the canyon in days.

The rocks came alive. "Beautiful," I said to Diego.

"*Magnifico*," he agreed.

"Keep it in your mind so you can describe it to your mother."

"Do you really believe I will see her again?" he whispered.

"Don't give up hope, Diego. One thing I promise you, we won't abandon you. You're staying with us."

He squeezed my hand. "Heads up!" I called to Rio. "Look, we're coming up on the narrows—Bullis Fold Rapid—and there's trees in the river."

"Got it," our boatman replied grimly.

This wasn't going to be easy. As the canyon walls narrowed to a bottleneck, the flooding river couldn't pass through without boiling chaotically back upon itself. There was no current line to follow downstream. I saw nothing but tremendous sucking whirlpools from wall to wall. To make it even worse, there were trees in the whirlpools, including huge cottonwoods.

Rio had to keep off those trees, and he knew it. The first whirlpool caught us, spinning us round and round, and he fought desperately to escape it. He did, only to be caught by another, more powerful whirlpool that was holding two cottonwoods.

Just when it appeared we would be crushed between the trees, Rio put his entire body into his strokes, pulling with everything he had and more. We were thrown spinning into yet another whirlpool. This was no Class 2. In a flood, these narrows could be every bit as deadly as the worst rapids.

Splayed across the blue tarp behind Rio, Carlos clung tenaciously to the straps across the load. Nothing was going to pry him loose.

What about his pistol—where was it?

Just inside his backpack, no doubt, clipped beside him. The backpack was unzipped at the top.

One by one, Rio put the whirlpools behind him. The last one threw us onto a current surging downstream at last. We rode it around a horseshoe bend, under a cave and some arches on the Texas side, and on to Palmas Rapid a mile below.

Palmas, rated a Class 2, wasn't even a 1. It was all washed out. On we sped to Rodeo Rapid at Mile 50.

Supposedly another Class 2, Rodeo looked like 4-plus. The right side was studded with boat-eating holes—huge boiling reversals on the downstream side of submerged boulders. Most of the river was pouring down the left side, against a steep slope of smooth rock. The wave train waiting below the entry had more standing waves in a row than I'd ever seen. From above the rapid, they looked taller than the raft was long.

Rio stood up on his seat to get the best possible view down the length of the rapid, sat back down, and announced we were going to run the big wave train down the left side. "Hang on!" he ordered as we raced down the tongue. "Dylan, you jump on the oars if I get blown out!"

"Don't even think of it!" I yelled. "You're not wearing a life jacket!"

This was going to be bigger than huge. I ran my hand through the harness we had rigged around Diego's waist and grasped the aluminum crossbar behind us.

Rio could have cheated this rapid, I knew, by taking a line just to the right of the wave train. I knew why he wanted to run the gut. He knew something that Carlos didn't: The ride was generally the wildest in the back. Sometimes in big water a raft tends to buckle just behind the boatman. When it buckles bad enough, the back of the raft becomes a catapult, and sends people flying.

No such luck. We took the huge ride through the troughs and over the tops of the crashing waves, Carlos yelling, *"Ole! Ole!"* all the way through.

Four fast miles below Rodeo, a landmark the guidebook told me to be on the lookout for suddenly appeared. Burro Bluff, on the Texas side, was unmistakable. Its sheer cliffs, where peregrine falcons nested, rose seven hundred feet from the river.

Here was the reason I was supposed to be keeping an eye out for Burro Bluff. At its foot lay Upper Madison Falls, "bad at any level."

I was sick to my stomach just hearing the roar as we drew near. "Dylan," Diego said anxiously, "what's that sound?"

"It's a big rapid, but don't worry. Rio's going to take us to shore before we get there so we can take a look at it."

"Which side does it say to portage on?" Rio called. His nerves were showing.

"It says, 'At high water, portage on the Mexican side.'"

"We'll see about that," Carlos yelled from the back of the raft.

"It says to land at the mouth of the side canyon, the *Cañon del Tule*," I instructed Rio, "just above the head of the rapid."

Rio ferried hard to the right side of the river. Landing there turned out to be impossible. The normally dry side canyon was flash flooding. There was no place to pull in. Did that mean we were going to have to run Upper Madison Falls without a chance to scout it? What chance would we possibly have?

I knew better than to speak. This very moment, Rio had to make a split-second decision. He had his eye on a small eddy on the Mexican side, just above the drop. Was it reachable? To get there, he would have to cut across the turbulent outwash from the flooding side canyon.

Rio pivoted decisively, and began to row hard across the crashing waves. If one of his oars so much as slipped out of his hand, there wouldn't be time to recover it. We would be swept down the right side of the rapid, which was choked with boulders big as Easter Island statues, impossible to run.

Rio won through his battle with the fast water. He pulled hard into the bottom of the eddy, swung the boat around, and bumped the shore front on. I leaped onto a ledge and tied the raft to a salt cedar.

Rio came off the raft with Diego and the guidebook. Carlos followed with his pistol in his waistband.

First thing Rio and I did was to see if we could locate the portage trail. "What are you guys doing?" Carlos called suspiciously.

"Looking for how to walk the raft around the rapid!" I hollered back.

We found neither a trail nor walkable ground. The portage route was underwater, completely flooded out. "We can wait here until the river goes down," I said to Rio, "even if there's not a place to camp. What's he gonna do, shoot us?"

Rio missed my lame attempt at a joke. "You know something I don't? Of course he would, and he'd start with you. Let's scout the rapid, see what we see."

The Deal Goes Down

RIO AND I CLAMBERED to the top of a high, flat boulder to see what we were up against. Upper Madison Falls looked nothing like the photo at low water in the mile-by-mile guide taken from high above, atop Burro Bluff. The photo showed the river dividing after the first drop into two rock-studded channels separated by an immense boulder field down the middle. The boulder field looked like an island of sorts.

In flood, the Upper Madison we were looking at was a whole different animal. It was huge and it was fast, with only a few rocks showing. Our problem wasn't rocks. Our problem—the ugliest, most lethal obstacle I'd ever seen in a river—was logs. Early in the rapid, at the head of the all-but-submerged island, a monumental logjam had formed. A tremendous amount of debris had been pinned there by the force of the current. At the base of the logjam were the trunks of several huge cottonwoods. At both ends of the logjam, limbs with bright green leaves were sawing up and down in the river.

I was sick at the thought of flying down off the top of the rapid directly at those pinned trees, and trying to row to one side or the other.

Rio was staring at the logjam with laserlike intensity.

Carlos climbed to the top of a nearby boulder. Above the roar of the rapid, he called to Rio, "What do you think, *Capitán*?"

Rio didn't answer. He kept staring at that logjam, and the whitewater pillowing off it.

After studying the logjam even longer, Rio turned to Carlos. "The portage trail is flooded out. We should wait right here for the river to go down."

"That would take days."

"Probably so. But that's what I say we should do. You just called me *Capitán*."

Carlos pulled his persuader from his waistband and waved it back and forth. "*Capitán, sí*, but I am *El Comandante*. Can't you go around one side of those logs or the other?"

"That logjam is going to come up real fast. If I lose control of an oar . . . do you have any idea what would happen if we got swept against those logs?"

"Tell me, Texas."

"The raft would flip over in a nanosecond. We'd all be thrown under the water. Guess what's underwater in a logjam like that."

"Tell me, Texas."

"Branches. The power of the current would pin our bodies underwater against the branches. The current has more force than you can imagine. That logjam is a death trap. Trees in the river are the worst hazard there is. Does that explain it for you?"

Carlos scratched the stubble on his jaw. "You still have no idea who you're dealing with, do you, Texas? I know what death looks like, and I am not afraid of it. There is only one thing that I fear, and that is prison. If I wait here like you say, I am going to prison. If we get in that boat, and you are rowing for your life with no life jacket, you are going to do your very best, and I will leave this river behind in a couple hours. We go our separate ways."

"You promise you'll let us live, then, and you'll leave Diego with us?"

"My little chicken, too? You drive a hard bargain, *El Capitán*!"

"Do you promise, or not?"

Carlos laughed. "*Sí, sí*, I promise, by all that is holy, including the grave of my mother."

What a farce, I thought. Why was Rio even bothering?

"Okay," Rio said grimly. "Let's run the sucker."

I was sick, just sick to the pit of my stomach. As I followed Rio down off the boulder, I knew all too well I might have only minutes to live. My head was ringing, my heart was pounding . . . I thought I was going to heave.

I stopped in my tracks, and that's exactly what I

did—bent over and puked. Nothing much came out of my mouth. I'd hardly been putting anything into it. I was wracked by wave after wave of dry heaves.

Finally it was over, and Rio was at my side. "Sorry, *primo*," I told him. "I lost it, I guess."

"I'm the one who's sorry."

"What for?"

"For getting you into this fix."

"I don't know what you're talking about."

"Sure you do. From the very beginning—"

"Rio," I said. "I knew the score. I knew what I was doing, and I've only got myself to blame."

"Hey!" Carlos roared. "You guys get over here!"

My cousin reached out and put his hand on my shoulder. "Now listen, Dylan. No time to explain, but I have something in mind. When I yell 'Jump,' you stay in the boat, and you keep Diego in the boat. *You don't jump*, got it?"

"Get over here now, you two!"

"I got it," I told Rio. "You stay in the boat, too, okay?"

"I promise. And thanks for everything, Dylan. You're true blue. It's been awesome running with you."

"Knock it off," I said. "We're going home with stories to tell."

Carlos glowered at us as we reached the boat. "What were you two doing back there?"

"Throwing up," I said.

He laughed cruelly. "Wipe your mouth. I can see that you were."

I helped Diego into the front of the raft. Still on the shore, Carlos hesitated. Thinking about where he was going to ride, I guessed.

Carlos tucked his pistol under his waistband, climbed aboard, and went to the back. He should have been afraid of losing his gun to the river in water this rough, but apparently it hadn't crossed his mind. It was time we caught a break.

It was easy enough to guess why he didn't want to ride up front with me and Diego. He thought I might try to shove him overboard in the heat of the action. He wanted things just as they were, with me up front taking care of Diego and him at the opposite end. I couldn't reach him and Rio couldn't see him.

Rio climbed in, took his seat, took a deep breath. He told me to untie, and to hold the boat at the shore until he was ready.

I did as I was told, taking a few deep breaths myself. I had to have faith in my cousin. Whatever he was up to, he had it under control. My job was to stay in the boat and make sure Diego did the same.

The boat was rocking like a racehorse ready to run as I held it and secured the coiled tie-rope around the grab line. "Now listen, everybody," Rio said. "Listen real good. Did everybody see that logjam?"

"I didn't," Diego said. "I was afraid to look."

Rio's chuckle was rueful. "That's just as well, Diego. Here's the deal. There's one really bad thing about this rapid—some logs in the middle of the river. Soon as we go over the edge, we're going to be heading right for them. I'm going to be pulling hard to go to whichever side of the logjam looks best. Probably toward the Texas side. If something happens—if I get tossed out or lose control of an oar—and we get swept against those logs, the boat will flip over."

"Texas, quit talking like that." Carlos scolded from his perch on the stern.

"Listen, there's something we can do if that happens. If the raft is swept against the logs, we have a chance to survive if we time it just right. If we're going to hit the logs, I'll yell 'Jump!' at the last second. If I yell 'Jump,' don't hesitate—the boat's gonna flip. We have to get onto the logs as fast as we can. That's our only chance. Jump on the logs and climb to the top of the pile."

"That's enough!" Carlos barked. "Get in the boat, Carolina. Let's get this over with."

"Not until Rio says he's ready," I fired back.

Rio took another deep breath. He closed his eyes. He exhaled.

"I'm ready," he announced softly. I wished he'd said it with more conviction.

I gave the raft a small push and climbed aboard. I made sure Diego's life jacket was cinched tight to his harness, and I checked my own cinches. Carlos saw me doing that and thought better of keeping his pistol in his waistband. He quickly stowed it in his backpack. By this time we were already at the head of the eddy and Rio was pulling into the current. There is only one word to describe that look that was back on Rio's face: *fierce.*

Rio Bravo Robbins, I thought. Be *bravo*, Rio. Be *bravo.*

Rio pulled hard to reach the middle of the flooding river. The sky was blue, I noticed, nothing but beautiful blue. Pretty quick we could see over the brink of the rapid to the logjam waiting below, not at all far below.

As we went over the brink, the flow narrowed and accelerated. It was all a blur, we were going so fast. The water got rough, waves crashing from both sides. Rio cocked the front of the boat toward the right side so he could start pulling to the left. He was going to try to clear the logjam on the Texas side, like he said.

The turbulence was worse than I'd ever seen, and the logjam was looming. I glanced back at Carlos. He was keeping low, hanging on with a death grip.

Rio kept fighting left and was making good progress, but suddenly the turbulence ripped the right oar from his hand. Instantly, the raft was out of control and we were in deadly trouble, closing on the logs at a high rate of speed. Rio reached forward for the oar handle. He managed to grab it and got back in his seat and starting rowing for all he was worth.

Rio had lost his angle. In the seconds it took to regain it, we were half again as close to the logs. Now he was pulling left again, but he wasn't going to make it. We were seconds from impact on the far left side of the log-jam. The trunks of the trees were dead ahead.

It looked like we were going to be swept into the logs

broadside, at the worst possible angle. The full length of the raft would take the hit, and if it did, it was going to flip just like Rio had said.

Diego tried to rise, to get ready to jump. It took every last bit of faith I had in my cousin not to get ready myself. I held Diego down. I made sure he wasn't going anywhere.

At the last possible second, with a mighty pivot, Rio spun the raft. I saw the back of the boat swinging around. It was the back the boat, and the back of the boat only, that was going to take the hit.

Carlos was in a crouch, backpack on his back, hanging on with both hands but poised to leap. *"Jump!"* Rio roared, a fraction of a second before the boat bumped the logs. Carlos leaped, and timed his leap well. He landed on one log and scrambled to the one above.

Along with the tremendous jolt we took, we got a terrific bounce. Rio dug hard with both oars, and we pinballed around the Texas side of the logjam, barely out of reach of a tree branch sawing up and down in the river. We were free of the logs and hurtling downstream through the fastest water I had ever seen. Rio and I looked over our shoulders to the receding logjam, where Carlos, who had whipped off his backpack, was reaching inside for his gun.

By the time he had it out, and was able to aim, two-handed, we were almost out of reach downriver where the canyon was bending left. "Get down!" Rio yelled, and all three of us went to the floor of the raft. Over the pounding whitewater, we heard the bursts of gunfire.

Soon as the firing ended, Rio climbed back into his seat and regained the oars. We turned the corner in the canyon and Upper Madison Falls disappeared from view. "We're free!" I hollered. "You faked him out, Rio! We're free, Diego! He can't touch us now!"

Rio had his hands full with another rapid, Lower Madison Falls. We took some whitewater over the bow, but it was all washed out—no rocks, no holes, no logs.

Below Lower Madison, the three of us were out of our minds with relief, whooping and hollering and jumping for joy. The adrenaline wasn't going to stop anytime soon. Rio let go of the oars and stood up on the rowing seat, doing a victory dance. I was pumping my fist and Diego was doing the same.

Rio dropped back into his seat, grabbed hold of the oars, and rowed hard for shore. We landed on a new-made sandbar and tied the boat three ways from Sunday to the trunk of a mesquite. Then we totally lost it. All that pent-up fear gave way, and we went crazy-wild throwing ourselves down, jumping up, and throwing ourselves down again. I lifted Diego up high, and he pumped both his fists. I put him down, and Rio grabbed him and swung him around and around. We both told him how incredibly brave he had been.

Shaggy hair flying, Rio ran to the end of the sandbar yelling, "I'm alive! I'm alive! I'm alive!"

Diego and I took up the chant, and we ran up and down the sandbar, too, yelling, "We're alive! We're alive! We're alive!"

I nearly had to tackle Rio to slow him down. There

was something I had to ask him. I barely had the breath. "Going into the logjam . . . did you lose control of the oar on purpose, because you told Carlos we'd be in huge trouble if you did?"

Rio, too, was heaving for breath. "That was the plan, and so was bumping the logs with the back of the boat, and faking him into jumping, but I didn't realize how little time there would be! When we were going into the logs broadside, I didn't know if I had enough time to spin the raft! I knew we'd be goners if I couldn't get that oar back fast and make the spin!"

"Desperate times call for desperate measures, and you pulled it off!"

Diego, we realized, was no longer celebrating. He was staring upriver so intensely I thought he had spied Carlos coming after us.

That's exactly what he was worried about. "Let's get going!" the boy pleaded. "He has a life jacket on! What if he comes after us?"

We told him that wasn't likely, given the ferocity of the whitewater he would have to jump into, but we couldn't be sure. We got back on the river and Rio started pulling for home. The takeout was twenty-five miles downstream. On this racehorse-fast current, we could get there before the day was done.

What the Chopper Saw

RIO KEPT THE RAFT in the fastest current, pushing hard for home. The sun was shining and the skies were blue. Eighteen miles below Lower Madison, we emerged from the towering Lower Canyons. The cliffs shrank to no more than a couple hundred feet high. There were cattle on both shores; this was ranching country. The ebbing river was already a couple feet down from the tops of the new sandbars it had created.

We counted up the days. It was hard to believe, but this was only our sixth. With just eight miles to go in our 116-mile journey, we had spent only five nights out. We had planned on nine. Ariel wasn't scheduled to meet us at the Dryden takeout until noon on the tenth day.

Was there any chance she might come sooner?

Most likely she would, we figured. She knew our ten-day schedule was based on low water.

Might she be at the takeout already?

The chances of that were south of unlikely.

Even so, we wanted to get off the river in the worst way. According to Rio, there was a fish camp at the takeout. He'd waited there for his dad to come off the river a couple of times. There might even be people there.

"What kind of amenities does this fish camp have?" I wondered aloud.

Taking a break from the oars, Rio reached for his water bottle. "It's got a ramada with a metal roof and no walls that makes shade for a bunch of picnic tables on a concrete slab. Off to the side, there's a fish-cleaning station and a barbeque grill. It has good, clean water that arrives via gravity feed from a holding tank next to a windmill. Anything else you wanted to know?"

"If we have to kill the next three or four days there, do you think we could catch some fish?"

"I don't see why not. We've got juglines and Zote Soap."

I asked Diego if fried catfish sounded good to him. He said it did. Rio said he thought we could also scare up a snake. Diego didn't think much of that idea. Rio said we could slow-roast a cow overnight, underground, if we could catch one. Diego smiled but he didn't laugh. Good try, I thought. Rio was trying to distract Diego from succumbing to the grief he was feeling over his father.

We still had a few rapids to run, Sanderson Canyon Rapid and Agua Verde Rapid. Rio had me take the oars for both. I slopped through with zero style points.

In the bottom of Agua Verde Rapid, we spotted the trail to the Mexican village a mile south. Rio and I exchanged glances, picturing all too well what would have happened to us here had he not been able to shake Carlos.

Pretty quick, we had our sights on the river gauge pictured in the guidebook. Only six or seven feet of pipe were showing between the instrument box under the solar panel and the river below. In the photo, the flow gauge was closer to thirty feet above the river. Rio couldn't wait to get home and find out how much water we'd been running on.

As we drifted by the gauge, our eyes went to the metal ramada downstream, the fish camp at the Dryden takeout. "You're on your way home," I said to Diego.

First thing, we walked up to the fish camp to see if Ariel might possibly be there. She wasn't. The place was deserted. Even though we weren't expecting any different, it was still a disappointment.

We returned to the raft for our gear. Rio said we wouldn't break down the raft until Ariel drove in. We would need it for setting out our juglines when the river slowed down enough that we could fish it.

We made supper as the sun was setting. We still had some soup packets and a box of mac and cheese. After supper we played Hearts. From the picnic table where we sat, we watched the bats begin to work the river. They included mastiff bats with wingspans nearly two feet across.

It got so dark we had to break out the candles to keep playing. I asked Rio if he thought the twenty-mile road from the highway to the river would be dry enough the next day, if Ariel got the notion, for her to come in and pick us up. He remembered it as caliche clay—no gravel—and said it would take at least another full day before anybody could drive in. We might have to go on that snake hunt he was talking about.

When it came to our sleeping arrangements, I inflated our two ground pads and announced that it was my turn to go without. "Deal," Rio agreed. I made do with a bed of cane tops, and arranged my sleeping sheet on top of that. At least I had something between me and the concrete.

It wasn't the most restful night of my life. The other two slept like the dead while I relived the events of the last couple days. It was impossible to get my mind off of Carlos. He was out there, and maybe he wasn't where we thought he was, stranded on the logjam and waiting for the river to go down. He might've swum off it, like Diego was thinking. Maybe he found another boat. He might be sneaking up on us in the dark.

It was exhaustion, finally, that shut down my over-worked imagination. I woke to the rising sun warm against my eyelids. Rio and Diego were still asleep. I got up and walked down to the river. It looked like it had dropped by half. I wondered if it might be fishable already. A beaver, of all things, was swimming upstream along the Mexican shore.

Two hours later Rio and Diego still weren't up, and

I was bored out of my skull. I was about to start making some coffee when I heard something. One second it wasn't there and the next second it was. "Chopper!" I yelled. Rio leaped to his feet and so did Diego. All three of us went running from the ramada into the open. I was expecting a Black Hawk.

The sound was coming from upriver. Here came the chopper. It wasn't black, and it wasn't military. It was red and white. I grabbed a life jacket off the gear pile and waved it wildly around my head. "That's Big Bend's chopper," Rio said. "Big Bend National Park."

The helicopter landed in the parking lot off to the side of the fish camp. When the rotors stopped turning, two men stepped out. Rio identified them for me before running to shake hands. The pilot, in a flight suit, was Tony Medina. The one in the Park Service uniform was Rob Baker, the Big Bend River Ranger.

I looked around for Diego. He had retreated to the shade of the ramada, where he was sort of hiding. I caught up with Rio, and I got huge handshakes, too.

"You guys," the pilot said. "You have no idea how good this feels."

"Oh yes, we do," Rio assured him.

"I flat-out don't believe that you're here!" exclaimed Rob, the River Ranger. "The takeout is the last place we expected to find you! You ran the river at the height of the storm?"

"I'm afraid so," Rio said. "How big did the water get?"

"It came close to topping the '58 flood. The Dryden

gauge peaked yesterday at forty-seven thousand six hundred cubic feet per second. The upper half of the Big Bend didn't get nearly the rain. The storm passed us by to the east, heading north—Terlingua got only an inch. It was the Lower Canyons that got hammered. You should've seen the satellite photo."

"Plumb ugly," the pilot chimed in. "This morning was the first time we could fly. The National Weather Service is estimating that the Lower Canyons got fifteen inches."

"I believe it," I chimed in. "It was something to see."

The River Ranger suddenly got all serious. "Here's what we need to know right now. Below San Rosendo, just past the cliff, we spotted a red canoe at the shoreline. Figured it must be your Mad River, Rio. When we got to Upper Madison, we saw a man in a life jacket sitting on top of the huge logjam in the middle of the rapid, and started wondering if the canoe was his. We have no idea who he is. He didn't fill out a permit. Did you guys run into him? We've called for a rescue chopper—do you have any idea who that is?"

"A murderer, a kidnapper," Rio replied, and pointed their attention to Diego, who had retreated to the farthest, darkest corner of the ramada.

Rio was only beginning to bring them up to speed when the pilot, who'd heard enough, ran to the chopper to get on the radio. Earlier, he had called for a search-and-rescue chopper. Now he had a warning to get out: The man on the logjam was an armed and dangerous Mexican national, the suspected kidnapper in the abduction of the judge's son at the lodge in the Sierra del Carmen.

We asked the River Ranger if he knew of the fate of Diego's father. "He was the only one of the three judges who survived," Rob said. "That's what the newspapers and TV and radio are reporting. His clerk sitting next to him got killed, but the judge was only wounded, and not critically. He was evacuated to a hospital in Mexico City, and is doing well. The other three hit men, by the way, were killed in a running gun battle, with the help of our Army Rangers. The manhunt for the fourth is still on. This is going to be big news, guys, huge news!"

Rio and I headed over toward Diego. "You've been like a big brother to him," Rio said. "You should be the one to tell him."

Diego was in the farthest corner of the ramada, where he sat at a picnic table with his head down. He lifted his head as we approached. Tears welling, he said, "Do they know anything about my father? Did they say anything?"

I sat down, put my arm around his trembling shoulders, and gave Diego the best news he could have imagined, so much more than he had dared to hope. "Your father is alive. He's in the hospital in Mexico City. He was hurt, but he's going to be fine."

It must have sounded too good to be true. I saw him fighting to shake off his disbelief. "Really," I said. "He's with your mother, and they're waiting for you."

Diego couldn't hold back the tears any longer. When they broke loose, they were tears of joy.

The D-Word

IEGO AND MY COUSIN and I climbed aboard the helicopter and we lifted off. The direct route to Terlingua
Ghost Town took us up the muddy brown river, over
the twists, turns, and horseshoe bends of the Lower Canyons. The river from above, winding through that deep
corridor of solid limestone, was a sight I would never forget.

As Tony Medina approached Upper Madison Falls, he
was flying well above the range of Carlos's weapon. I had
a window seat, and was keeping my eyes peeled for the
fugitive. I spotted Lower Madison Falls, and pretty soon
we were over Upper Madison.

The logjam was still there, at the head of the island
that was submerged only the day before. Overnight, with
the water receding, dozens of boulders had popped up like
dragons' teeth.

My eyes went back to the logjam. Where was Carlos? Granted, I wasn't looking through binoculars like the River Ranger was, but I didn't really need them. I should have been able to spot the orange life jacket or the white shirt. I saw only logs and debris. Carlos had been on those logs within the hour, and now he was gone.

Rio and Diego and I had headsets that enabled us to hear what Tony and Rob were saying. Fifty minutes earlier, the suspect knew he'd been spotted. He even waved back. When the helicopter continued downstream, he knew it would soon come across us. He decided to jump in the river and try his chances in the rapids rather than wait for capture.

For the next fifteen minutes we backtracked, buzzing three or four miles of the canyon below the logjam, but failed to spot him.

The search-and-rescue helicopter showed up and hovered a few hundred yards away from us. We listened to the chatter back and forth. The other pilot was going to continue the search but attempt no rescue. Law enforcement and the armed forces on both sides of the border would be joining in. The search-and-rescue pilot said to tell the judge's son that the Mexican consulate in El Paso had already been notified that Diego was soon to arrive in Terlingua Ghost Town. His parents would be hearing soon if they hadn't already.

Diego was sitting right across from me. Despite the radio crackle, he understood. He was positively glowing. Rio and I reached out, and the three of us clasped hands.

Tony wished the other pilot good hunting and we flew upriver. It wasn't long before I was looking down at the Hallie Stillwell Bridge and the abandoned village of La Linda. There was the white church with the twin bell towers we had seen from the river.

A few minutes after that, as we passed over the downstream mouth of Boquillas Canyon, I spotted the wax makers working at their vat, and their burros. Before long we left the canyon behind, and the village of Boquillas came into view. Here we left the river and made a beeline for Terlingua Ghost Town.

We landed only a couple blocks from the Starlight Theatre, on a basketball court. Half-court to be exact. The hoop was askew and missing a net. This is where Rio and I would have spent our time shooting hoops if we had bailed out at the bridge instead of forging ahead into the Lower Canyons. I shuddered to think what would have become of Diego.

Rio climbed out of the chopper, then me. I turned around to catch Diego, and planted him on terra firma. Rob told us to check in with Ariel first thing. She had been following the storm on her computer, and was worried sick about us. We promised we would, said our thank-yous and good-byes, and waved to our friends as they lifted off.

In the heat of late morning, the ghost town was pretty much deserted. Rio and I got a few waves as we walked past the Starlight, river bags over our shoulders and Diego in tow. I got the idea that seeing Rio come off a river trip was nothing new around the ghost town. Unlike Ariel, those Terlinguans who just waved had no notion that we had gotten personally acquainted with Dolly. It was just as well. We didn't want to stop and talk. All we wanted was to get clean and find something to eat.

We trudged up the hill, passing Rio's driveway by in favor of Ariel's. Her bus came into view, and we quickened our steps. There she was, painting in the shade of her ramada.

We were halfway down her driveway when Ariel looked up and saw what might have been the filthiest, most banged-up trio ever to come off the Rio Grande. She shrieked and came running, paintbrush in hand. We were soon smothered with hugs and kisses and daubed with red paint. Our Terlingua homecoming couldn't have been sweeter.

"Did you meet a new friend on the river?" Ariel asked, meaning Diego. "Don't tell me—I've seen his face before."

In a second, she had it. She'd seen a picture of Diego on TV, on the Midland/Odessa station. She was beside herself. Right behind us, a Jeep pulled into Ariel's driveway. It was her friend Yolanda from the Terlingua Trading Company. Yolanda fussed over the three of us, wanting to hear all about it. Through the trading post window, she had seen us get out of the Big Bend helicopter. She didn't rush out to greet us because she had just taken a call from the Mexican consulate in El Paso. She was on hold, waiting for the consul himself to pick up. Finally he did. The consul told her he would be arriving in three hours to pick up Diego Cervantes, the boy who had been kidnapped and was being flown to the ghost town.

"Clothes!" Yolanda cried. "The boy needs clean clothes."

"And a meal—for the three of them," Ariel added.

"And hot showers," I chipped in.

The showers we would take care of at Rio's. The clothes search would begin with a family that had a seven-year-old boy. A lady named Georgene was going to fix us lunch. Georgene owned the Lost Lizard B&B just down the street and always kept a full refrigerator. She had the best patio in town and loved to feed people.

Yolanda left in a hurry to get Georgene started on lunch. Ariel made a successful call to the ghost town mother who had the seven-year-old boy. We headed around Ariel's back fence for home and those hot showers.

There was no one there to greet us but Roxanne. When Diego saw her, he about jumped out of his skin. Once they were properly introduced, he was cool with it. He hadn't known that tarantulas are harmless.

I'm going to fast-forward to two o'clock that afternoon, when the Mexican consul arrived from El Paso. The U.S. Army brought him on a medevac helicopter, not that Diego needed a medical evacuation. When the consul stepped out of the helicopter, he got a rousing ovation from a crowd of more than fifty. News travels fast in a small town.

The consul got a welcoming speech from the owner

of Terlingua Ghost Town. Who knew that the ghost town had an owner? Everybody but me and Diego, apparently. The consul, a dignified man with flowing white hair and a full white mustache, gave a brief yet eloquent speech. It ended to applause and whoops and hollers when he shook Rio's hand and mine. This was a bit much for Rio. Some of his high school buddies had somehow heard what was up, and had raced from far-flung corners of the county to be there. "Speech, Rio!" they chanted. My cousin would've crawled under a rock if there'd been one handy.

Pretty quick, we were saying good-bye to Diego. He called us his *hermanos*—his brothers. He said he would never forget, and that his family would always be grateful. He hoped that Carlos didn't drown, that he would soon be caught, and that his worst nightmare—life in prison—would come true.

Diego waved from the open door of the helicopter. He was wearing jeans and a Terlingua Youth Soccer shirt that pictured a skeleton-kid dribbling a ball off his knee. He gave Rio and me two quick fist pumps and one more wave good-bye.

As the chopper lifted off, the whole crowd was waving. There wasn't a dry eye to be seen. Rio and I were still wiping tears when Rio was mobbed by his friends and a young woman named Amanda from KYOTE Coyote Radio.

Who knew that the ghost town had a radio station? Everybody but me. Amanda wanted an interview, and she wanted it now. She had her tape recorder in hand, and her microphone was at the ready. "How 'bout sunset?" Rio said. "Right here on the porch." He told her he had promised to call his dad in Alaska on this date and right around this time, which turned out to be true. His father was in between his first and second trips on the Alsek River, and had arranged the call with Rio shortly after arriving in Alaska, not that Rio had ever mentioned it to me.

"I'm going to have to take some lumps," Rio said. "Me not telling you and your family, like I was supposed to, that he wasn't even going to be here, that's not going to go over so good."

"How about the river trip? Is he going to be as cool with that as you thought?"

"Maybe not," Rio allowed, and went into the Starlight to make his call.

I had a call of my own to make, and lumps to take. I called from next door, at the Terlingua Trading Company. Naturally I was hoping that nobody would pick up, and I could leave a message. Guess who answered. That's right, my mother.

Where do I even start? I asked myself. I began with a cheerful "I just got back from the river!"

"Did you guys have a good time?"

"Incredible!"

"How'd you like your uncle Alan?"

I held my breath. The clock was ticking. "Uh, actually, he was in Alaska."

It went downhill from there. The next subject that

came up was the weather. Back home, they'd been worrying about Dolly. "Were you anywhere near the storm when it brushed the Big Bend?"

"Actually, Mom, we were right in it. We got back early because the river was so high and so fast."

Were any of the rapids dangerous, she wanted to know.

Only the one with a logjam in it, I told her.

"Did you know there was a violent incident near the Big Bend, in the mountains in Mexico?"

"Uh . . . not until we ran into the kidnapper . . . and the boy who got kidnapped."

Well, that's all I'm going to say on the subject of this phone call. It lasted about an hour, and I did some serious apologizing. My mom used the D-word—*disappointed*—five or six times. That about killed me. She forgave me before it was over, though, but only because I'd lived through it in one piece.

Bringin' It All Back Home

ARIEL HAD HER RADIO dialed to KYOTE Coyote Radio when Amanda came on the air with the intro to her interview with Rio. Ariel and I were listening in from her place, under the ramada. "Just be yourself," Ariel had told him.

It must have helped that Rio's buddies weren't there watching him. It was just Rio and Amanda in the station's tiny space in the building behind the Terlingua Trading Company, and he hit it out of the park. I wished my parents could've heard the interview. They would've discovered how golden he was, and how well he handled himself.

We spent the next day with Ariel recovering the raft and the rest of the gear we'd left at the takeout. A day and a half of desert sunshine had dried the road out enough for us to get through. Halfway down to the river we encountered a sheriff's department roadblock. The fish camp was off-limits until the manhunt was over. When we told them who we were and what we were after, they escorted us to the river. The sheriff scooped us with an update: Carlos hadn't been found, but his backpack had, with his weapon inside. The backpack had been discovered between Upper and Lower Madison, caked in mud, when the floodwater subsided. "Evidently he wasn't able to hang on to it as he swam the rapids and tried to get to shore," the sheriff said.

We asked if there was any indication that Carlos was alive. The sheriff thought long and hard before answering. "Can't say," he replied. To our mind, that was a yes.

As we loaded up our stuff, a couple of helicopters were working the area. We could pretty well guess that the United States and Mexico had boots on the ground as well. Carlos was probably hiding in some rat hole, waiting them out. We weren't very confident that he was going to get caught.

Late afternoon, as we drove into the ghost town and laid eyes on the Starlight, we knew something was up. The parking lot was packed, and it included a number of white vans with satellite dishes. "Hmmm . . .," I said. "What's this all about?"

"Rio's radio interview, bet you anything," Ariel said.

Rio had Ariel try to sneak her pickup past the Starlight, but they were on the lookout for us. Somebody pointed, and somebody else yelled, and suddenly we had a pack of media types on our heels.

"You might as well enjoy it," Ariel told my cousin. "It's going to be great for the ghost town. Think of the gas that's going to get sold, and the meals, and the rooms, and the art, and the souvenirs!"

"I'd rather run Upper Madison again," Rio groaned.

"Really?" I said.

"Not really . . . I can handle this . . . I can handle this . . . but you have to help me, Dylan."

"As long as you're the front man," I told him.

I had the passenger window down, and was taking in the sights and the sounds. This was unbelievable. A couple guys with big video cameras on their shoulders were already filming. I suppose Ariel's old truck with the oars and the raft frame lashed to the overhead racks was just the sort of material they were looking to shoot. We found out later they'd been filming around the ghost town all afternoon, killing time making "B roll" while waiting for us to get back.

We never even made it home. Covered with road dust and wearing our beat-up straw hats from the river, we did three interviews in the next two hours. The first was with the Midland/Odessa station, the second was with the El Paso station, and the third was with the San Antonio station. It turned out that the interviewers, and the crews, too, had all been in Terlingua Ghost Town before, covering the annual world-famous chili cook-offs. They were huge, apparently.

The TV reporters all wanted their interview to take

place on Terlingua's world-famous porch, with the Chisos Mountains in the background.

That's where we did them, out in front of the Starlight. With my sunglasses to hide behind, it wasn't that bad. Rio kept pulling me in. What could I do?

The sweetest part was ending up the last interview as sunset was lighting up the battlements of the Chisos Mountains. I was saying how much I loved the ghost town, and the Big Bend, and the river. That I'd be back first chance I got.

Then it was over. They told us we would be on the late news in about an hour. We headed into the Starlight; all we cared about was supper. The place was packed, just jumping. A cowboy band was playing. There was a line to get seated, but they brought us right in, me and Rio and Ariel. Yolanda and Georgene and Amanda were waiting at a reserved table. We got a round of applause. This was crazy!

The owner of the Starlight came over, shook our hands, and said that everything was on the house. We ordered the biggest steaks they had. While we were waiting, the cowboy band called Rio up to sing with them.

The song Rio sang was that old Marty Robbins tune, "El Paso," one of my all-time favorites. In the very first line, Rio dropped "El Paso" and replaced it with "Terlingua," so it went like this: *"Out in the West Texas town of Terlingua, I fell in love with a Mexican girl . . ."*

Rio knocked the place dead. When he sat down I asked

him if it was true about the Mexican girl. "Not tellin'," he replied.

It was ten thirty by the time we got home. We were sitting up talking about the river when Yolanda knocked on the door a half hour later. My parents had called, and they wanted me to call back.

Hmmm . . . , I thought. Back in Asheville, it's midnight. I bet they've decided against letting me hang here uncle-less for three more days, and go home on the day I was ticketed for.

Over at the Trading Company, I punched up home with more than a little apprehension. Here's what my parents wanted to talk about: Rio's interview with KYOTE in Terlingua, Texas. Turns out KYOTE Coyote Radio was an affiliate of National Public Radio, and my parents always listen to NPR. Rio's interview played in Asheville a few hours ago, and they'd heard the whole thing. Rio was fantastic, and all was forgiven. Rio sounded so mature, they said, and so modest. He never came out and said it, but we had saved the judge's son!

My mother had something else to tell me. Soon after the interview, her brother called from Alaska. Uncle Alan hadn't heard the interview but she filled him in on it. They had a long talk about the two of us and what we'd done. They decided we were stand-up guys, even though we were also numbskulls.

My mom told me that both of them were tempted to rush to Terlingua ASAP, but decided against it. They thought we should have the full time together that my plane ticket allowed. Not only that, they were talking about my whole family coming out to the ghost town in late October for the chili cook-offs and the Day of the Dead. The weather was always perfect then, and my mother would love the Lost Lizard B&B. Her brother was guaranteeing that it was scorpion proof.

"So, are we really going to do it?" I asked my mom. "Come out to Terlingua this fall?"

"That's what I'm trying to tell you," she said. "I'm overdue, as you know."

Things were looking up. Way up.

It wasn't hard to kill the next three days. We put a lot of miles on Rio's mountain bike and his dad's. I still had that hundred dollars I hadn't taken on the river, and it was burning a hole in my pocket. I stopped by the quilt shop to see if they had any quilts made by the women of Boquillas del Carmen. They had dozens. I picked one out for my mother and had it shipped home.

I tried to track down another souvenir from Boquillas, something for myself. On the river, Rio had mentioned that in addition to quilts, Fronteras Unlimited also imported walking sticks from Boquillas as well as scorpions made of copper wire. I struck out on both counts. The TV crews had snatched them all up. Oh well, I could look for them in the fall.

On my last day we hiked to the brink of Santa Elena Canyon, lay on our bellies, and looked eight hundred feet straight down to Rock Slide Rapid. From above, I wouldn't have thought it was runnable. Rio said it wasn't as bad as it looked. We talked about paddling it in the fall.

On my fly day, we had to get up early to catch my eight AM bus out of Alpine. The sun was rising over the Chisos Mountains as Ariel drove us north. The big open desert sprinkled with mountains no longer looked like the far side of the moon. With Alpine in our sights, I spied a sign that said DON'T MESS WITH TEXAS. I got the threatening tone but couldn't make out what it actually meant, so I asked. My cousin got a good laugh out of that. He explained that it was the Lone Star State's antilitter motto.

Pretty soon we were standing on the curb in front of the High Desert Hotel, waiting for the Greyhound to lope into town. Rio asked me what the little cardboard box in the top of my backpack was all about. I said there was no such animal in my backpack as far as I knew. He said I should check.

I did, and I found a small box like he said I would. Inside was a wicked-looking scorpion fashioned from copper wire, cleverly braided. Its stinger was curled up and ready to strike. The eyes were made of small blue beads. "Awesome," I said, holding it out on my palm. Rio beamed.

There was more to come. Ariel had a bright-colored Guatemalan bag over her shoulder. She gave it to me and said the bag was for my mother. "Look inside," Rio said.

"What's inside the bag is for you," Ariel added.

Here came the bus. I had just enough time to undo the bubble wrap and see what this present was all about.

It was one of her hubcaps, with brightly colored geometric designs surrounding a canyon scene, a bird's-eye view of the Lower Canyons. There were two boats way down there on the winding river. One was a blue raft, and the other was a red canoe.

I just lost it. So did they.

All too soon the driver was throwing my duffel in the baggage compartment. We said our good-byes and our see-you-soons. I boarded the bus and took a seat on their side of the street. I had time to give them two fist pumps in honor of Diego before the bus blasted off in a cloud of diesel.

I have only one more thing to report. At the airport in El Paso, there was a headline in the newspaper that grabbed my attention on the way to the gate. It went like this: FUGITIVE CAPTURED ALIVE IN MEXICAN DESERT.

The story included a photograph of Carlos snarling like a rabid dog. It came as no surprise when I saw that his name wasn't Carlos. One of Mexico's 10 Most Wanted was on his way to prison.